Also by Lucinda McFall

Table of Contents

Big Package for Bunny

An opposites-attract romance

...and a parrot
Book 2 in the

series

Lucinda McFall

Shrike Publications

Albuquerque   Minneapolis

Shrike Publications

Albuquerque NM

Minneapolis MN

https://lucindawritesromance.com

Publisher's Note: This is a work of fiction. Names, characters, places, and incidents are a product of the author's imagination. Locales and public names are sometimes used for atmospheric purposes. Any resemblance to actual people, living or dead, or to businesses, companies, events, institutions, or locales is completely coincidental.

Book Layout ©2017 BookDesignTemplates.com[1]

Big Package for Bunny/ Lucinda McFall.—1st ed.

ISBN 979-8-9876660-3-6

To all the one-of-a-kind people we love to love, especially you parrot people.

All of the three books in the **Love's a Beach** series may be read stand-alone. If you read them out of order, though, the second two in the series will give you spoilers. Just saying.

See them all, and more romance by Lucinda McFall, at https://lucindawritesromance.com

She was not quite what you would call refined. She was not quite what you would call unrefined. She was the kind of person that keeps a parrot.

—Mark Twain, *Following the Equator*

Not my parrot

BUNNY JERKED BACK. She near-about stabbed herself with the pair of scissors she was about to use on the packing tape. Something inside the big package was making noise. The box began rocking from side to side.

She stared at the thing where it hulked on the tiny café table in her kitchen. "This doesn't look like the package I ordered. What's in there?" Her voice quavered.

Wondering if she should call someone, she backed away from the table and the thing on it. Shouldn't spooky music be playing in the background at times like these?

Bingo, Bunny's black lab, leaped about the kitchen, barking furiously. Not a fan of the package.

"Bingo. Sit," Bunny commanded.

Bingo, good dog, sat.

Gingerly Bunny stepped to the box, slit it open along the taped seam, and lifted the flaps.

She jumped back with a little scream.

WTF.

It was a parrot.

The creature cocked its head at her and emitted a loud SCRAW.

Bingo started barking again. Bunny forced the flaps back down as the parrot clawed to get out.

Her heart pounding, she fell onto the little wire-backed chair at the café table. Bingo nuzzled under her elbow to give her a reassuring dog kiss.

No no no no no.

"Bingo. Stay." In a flash, Bunny was at her front door, flinging it open, looking right and left up and down the beach.

"Hellooooo??" she tried.

Where was that delivery guy?

Around the back, the alley that ran behind her house, she heard the startup of a motor.

She whisked around the side of her house. The delivery guy was already in his van, already backing out of the alley and into the street.

"Wait!"

All the way across the broad back yard, he didn't see her. He drove away.

Damn.

She darted back into her house, grabbed her keys and purse. She eyed the carton on her café table, where it was rocking back and forth, a furious scrabbling coming from inside.

She hauled the thing up and tottered out to the driveway, where the hotpinkmobile broiled under the summer sun. Not even 9 am and already the weather was sweltering. And today, no beach breeze ruffled her hair. The air was absolutely still.

Juggling the box and her keys, she got the passenger-side door open, wincing as the hot metal of the door handle stung her. She eased the carton onto the seat.

Then she slung herself into the driver's seat, wiped the sweat from her eyes— *No, dear.* Her Aunt Fanny's voice in her head.

Women sweat. LADIES dew. –and sped out toward the highway and the UPackWeDeliver.

She screeched up to the entrance, parked, and went in. The young girl in the tan shorts and shirt at the counter looked her over, a bored expression plastered on her face. The AC was blasting in there, not that anyone could tell.

"Yeah? Help you?"

"You must be new." Bunny wiped the sweat from her forehead. She knew every single person in Currituck Cove, North Carolina, but she'd never laid eyes on this girl.

"Got sent over from Elizabeth City. They're short-handed here," said the girl. "Three people in this office here, they up and quit. So here I am. Help you?"

"One of your guys delivered a parrot to my house just now."

The girl's eyes lit. "Oh, yeah. The parrot. How's he doing? Doing okay? We were worried about him."

"I don't know how he's doing," said Bunny. "I have no idea." She waved her hand impatiently, feeling a little frantic. "He's not my parrot."

"Oh," the counter girl said. She worked her wad of gum a bit.

"He's in the car. Where can I put him?"

"Uh, we don't have the facilities to take care of a parrot, ma'am. That's why we were worried. We have to get live animals to their destinations right away, and today, it's hot, you know? We get 'em, we deliver them within the hour. It's in the manual."

"Not my problem," said Bunny, trying to stay calm. "Not my parrot."

"Uh," said the girl. She got down a thick book from a shelf and began leafing through it.

Behind Bunny, a little bell rang as the office door shoved open.

The girl looked up. She smiled past Bunny. "Hey, Finn! This lady has a problem with the parrot."

"Look," said Bunny, starting to feel desperate. "It's a big package. Can someone help me get it in here?" She glanced over her shoulder and her jaw dropped. She shut her mouth fast.

The guy who had just come into the office—Finn, the girl called him—was drop-dead and yes, jaw-dropping gorgeous. When he'd delivered the carton, she hadn't noticed. *That's not like me,* Bunny thought, her eyes roving up and down Finn. *I'd notice something like this.* She guessed she had been too excited about the delivery to pay much attention to the person who delivered it. My cosmetics supplies!

She'd signed Finn's form, and he'd dumped the carton on the front porch. *Leaving me to get that big package inside by myself.* She scowled at him.

He scowled back.

"You left the parrot in your car?" he said to Bunny.

"It's a big package," Bunny said defensively. "I could hardly shove it inside my house. You just plunked the thing down on my front porch. Then you drove away before I could wave you down. I had to work to get that big package out of my house again and to my car. I had to make a big effort to bring it back here. It's not my parrot." Now she narrowed her eyes. She didn't much like this Finn guy's attitude, square manly jaw or not. Hot body in hot tan shorts or not.

"It's a hot day, ma'am," Finn said to her in the patient voice you'd use to explain something to a toddler. "Parrots can get heat-stressed in a hurry. They dehydrate fast. You can't leave a parrot in a hot car."

Hot, Bunny's man-candy radar pinged. She made an impatient little gesture, shooing it away. There was a parrot, and it was in her car. "Get the parrot out of my car," Bunny said between tight lips. "Now."

Finn looked down at a clipboard he was carrying. He ran a ball-point pen down a list fastened to it. "You Bernice Dowdy?"

"Bunny," said Bunny. She knew everyone in this town. Why didn't she know Finn? Or the girl?

"Sorry, ma'am, if you're Bernice Dowdy, you're the recipient of the package." He shrugged. "We delivered it, and you took possession. You signed for it."

"It's not—" Bunny puffed out a breath. "my parrot."

"Here's your signature, right here." Finn held out the clipboard for her to see.

"I was expecting a different package. That's what I thought I was signing for." She stopped. This was going nowhere. "I'd like to speak to the manager."

"He's in Elizabeth City," said the girl at the counter.

"Someone needs to get the parrot out of my car."

"Sorry, ma'am," said Finn, with an infuriatingly polite smile. "We're not allowed to take a package back once the recipient has taken possession."

"It's in the manual," put in the girl behind the counter.

"But ma'am," Finn continued. "You need to get the parrot out of that hot car. Maybe take him back to your house? He needs water."

"If that parrot dies, that'll be on you," said Bunny in a constricted voice.

"No, ma'am," said Finn politely. "It'll be on you."

"You can fill out this form," said the girl behind the counter. "Bring it back here, or mail it to the address on the top, and one of our representatives will get back to you."

"Y'all are new to town. I can tell," said Bunny, grabbing the form and storming out to her car.

But when she slid into the driver's seat of the hotpinkmobile, the sun was blazing through the windshield, and the carton on the passenger seat was very still.

In a panic, she got herself back to her house and wrestled the carton into the AC. She hoisted it back onto her café table in her kitchen. With trembling fingers, she undid the flaps as Bingo lay whining softly on the cool tiles of the kitchen floor, thumping his tail.

The parrot was hunched in a corner.

Bunny licked her lips. Water. That's what those rude, rude people said he needed.

She ran a glass from the tap and reached it down into the carton, giving a little scream as the parrot made scrabbling noises with his claws.

They'd called him a "he," so Bunny guessed he must be a guy parrot.

"Hi," she told him, inching closer and peering over the top into the carton.

Damn. Why hadn't she noticed the air holes when she signed for the damn carton? She was too excited to get her shipment of cosmetics materials. She hadn't paid enough attention, and now look.

But the parrot was leaning over the water, and he was drinking it. Then he bustled around in the carton, and the water glass went over.

Damn.

He tilted his head up at her and moved it from side to side. He screamed.

Bunny jumped back. Damn!

She did the flaps back up, in case he got out and flew around.

Then she groped in her big purse and brought out the form those rude UPackWeDeliver people had handed her. The type was tiny. She groped around some more and extracted her readers, perching them on the end of her nose.

She got herself a cup of coffee from her Keurig machine. Put it into her favorite mug, one her friend Fran had given her last Christmas. *I got a GOOD HEART but THIS MOUTH*, the mug read.

Taking a sip, she peered at the form. RETURNS, said the headline at the top.

"Good, good," Bunny muttered.

Remove shipping label from carton and affix in the box below, the form read.

Bunny bent down to search for the shipping label on the side of the carton. Another scream from inside it made her grit her teeth. Bingo let out a short, sharp bark.

There. There was the shipping label, beside another big one, big red letters, LIVE ANIMALS.

Her mouth gaped open. The shipping label read, *Ms. Bernice Dowdy*. Then her address in Currituck Cove, North Carolina: *5 Beachcomber Road*. She was sure she was going to see some completely different address, some completely different addressee. Mr. Hot Pants—"Finn!" she gritted—must have gotten her address from some list, probably the one with her actual delivery on it, and delivered this box instead. Surely he must have.

But no. There on the side of the carton was her own address.

"Where are my cosmetics materials?" Bunny raged aloud.

She peered at the side of the carton again.

Back to the form.

We regret no returns on the following items.

Bunny ran her beautifully French-manicured finger down the list.

Livestock/live animals

"This. Is not." Her voice rose. The parrot's inside the carton rose with it. "My parrot!"

Watermelon man

"MISS BUNNY DOWDY, AS I live and breathe!" Joe Chasin, the hardware store clerk smiled big. "Haven't seen you in a age. What can I do for you, darlin?"

"Hey, Joe." Rude to rush him without asking about the family, but Bunny was in a state of near-panic. "Do you carry bird cages?"

"I think Mr. Fountain's gotta have just about one of everything in here, Bunny. If we do have one—not saying we do, but if—it'll be on the far wall." Joe gestured behind him with his thumb.

"Thanks, Joe."

As Bunny hustled to the back of the place, loaded with mer-chandise—pots and pans, cleaning supplies, big bags of dogfood, big bins of chickenfeed, crab traps and trotlines, bathing suits, big bags of candy, you name it—Joe began dealing with a delivery that had come in after her.

"Okay, thanks," she heard Joe saying. "So here? I sign here?" And then, "On the back wall. Yessir, just dump 'er back there and we'll figure out where to put 'er."

Bunny suppressed a giggle. Everything that didn't have an as-signed place in Fountain Feed and Seed went on its back wall. She remembered being a little kid, coming in here. All the kids knew to head for the back wall. That's where the treasures were. That sequined pair of flip-flops. . .Bunny's smile grew nostalgic for her twelve-year-old self.

She snapped to. Her eyes focused gimlet-style. There. Bird cage. She reached for it where it sat tilted over on a high dusty shelf, aware out of the corner of her eye that some guy with a hand-truck had begun unloading something beside her.

She couldn't quite reach. . .

"Uh, 'scuse me, but could you. . ." she said aside.

A big male presence stepped around her, getting the bird cage down for her.

"Thank you so much!" she gushed, reaching for it.

The man pulled it away.

She gaped up at him. "Finn."

"This isn't for the parrot, is it?"

She practically felt her hackles rise. It was rude Mr. Hot Pants, and now she knew what pissed her off even more. His voice. His accent. Why, he was a Yankee. "Yes. It's for the parrot. I can't keep the parrot in that carton. I need something to put him in while I find a home for him." She rounded on the man, furious. "Did you know. Did you know I can't return that thing? It's a live animal. No returns."

He took a quick step back, but he didn't let go of the bird cage. "Not our problem. That's the shipper's rule," he mumbled.

"Nothing is ever your problem. Not our problem. Not my department," she mimicked, getting madder by the minute. "You know how sick customers are of that kind of an attitude? I know. I was in sales, and I was good at it, too."

He stood staring at her, dumbstruck.

"Please hand over the bird cage."

"No."

"No?' Bunny prided herself on her kind, even temperament. But now for the third or fourth time in the same day, she found her voice rising up to screech-level.

"Ma'am. Uh. Ms. Dundy."

"Dowdy," she hissed.

"Ms. Dowdy, you can't keep that parrot in a cage like this."

She tilted her head at it. Bird cage. Pet birds lived in bird cages, didn't they? Her old Aunt Fanny had two canaries, and this is what they lived in. The cage was wire, it had a perch, it curved up into a kinda beehive shape, it had a little ring on top where it could hang from a stand. What the flack?

"It's not big enough for a parrot. What kind of parrot is it, anyway?"

"The green kind," she told him. Then she hated him more because she saw he was trying to suppress a grin. "You," she said, pointing a finger at him, poking it in fact against his chest, which felt rock-solid under the sexy tan jungle-explorer shirt they made these guys wear, "are an interfering son of a gun, aren't you?"

"I've been called worse," he admitted. "I really don't mean to interfere, but I know a lot about parrots, and this cage is 'way too small for a parrot, unless it's a really small parakeet. Not even then, probably." He looked down at her out of the most amazing green eyes she thought she'd ever seen.

Not parrot green. But really green.

"Judging from that carton I delivered, your parrot is much bigger than a parakeet."

"It's not my—" Bunny began. She wound down. "Uh. So. What kind is it?"

"What does it look like?"

"It's green, but it has some kinda blue-gray on it."

"Does it look like this?" Finn whipped out his cell phone, punched something in, and held it out for her to see.

"Yes!" Bunny screeched. "That's my parrot! He has that orange on him, too."

"He's a Senegal, then," said Finn. "Or she." At her look, he said apologetically, "It's hard to tell what sex they are. You can pay for a DNA test on him, to make sure."

"You're calling him a him," Bunny pointed out. "How sexist is that?"

"Busted," said Finn, and then he really did grin. A lock of dark hair flopped adorably over his forehead.

Bunny tried to hate him and failed. "That's stupid," she said instead. "How does anyone know what to name their bird, then?"

"Unisex name?" he ventured.

"Okay, Mister Know-It-All. Where do I find the right cage for him," Bunny demanded.

He winced. "Sorry. I just happen to know a lot—"

"—about parrots," she finished for him.

"You could order one online, or go to a really good pet store."

"This is a small town. You're not from around here," she said. "You must live in Elizabeth City." *But you're not FROM there*, she thought, her eyes narrowing suspiciously.

"Right now I do. I do live there. Temporarily." He looked at her sidelong, as if she might leap up and bite him. Or poke him again. "Elizabeth City has a couple nice pet stores. The big box kind, and one smaller specialty one, I think."

"Okay, then," said Bunny. "I'm naming him Buffet."

Mr. Hotpants rolled his eyes.

"Or, no—I know," she said, thinking of her last trip to New Orleans, back when she was working for the cosmetics company and they were rewarding her sales acumen with fancy trips. "I'm naming him Sazarac."

Finn nodded his head. "Now that I like," he said.

Bunny tossed her blonde curls. Who cared what he liked? She liked it. The parrot would like it. She was sure of that.

"So," he said. "You're getting him a cage. You've just named him. Looks like you're keeping him. Looks like he really is your—"

Before he could finish, Bunny flounced back to the front of the store.

"Find a bird cage?" said Joe Chasin.

"It's not the right size," said Bunny. "Bye-bye, now, Joe, you have a nice day, you hear?"

"Bye, sugar."

She got into the hotpinkmobile, and then she drove off a bit too fast toward the highway. Just a bit.

She headed toward Elizabeth City.

Before getting herself to the PetParade, she stopped for coffee with Fran, one of her two best friends. Fran had recently married her long-time suitor Nelson, and moved from Currituck Cove to Elizabeth City. Somehow, Bunny didn't bring up the parrot. She wasn't sure why. Too many complications, maybe. "Over here to do a little shopping," she said, waving her hands airily about.

Fran made them both nice mugs of coffee. She kept a special mug for Bunny's visits. *Classy, Sassy, and a Bit Smart Assy*, it read. Fran's own mug read *49% Banker, 51% Badass*. Fran had retired from banking, but not from this mug.

At the PetParade, Bunny bought a nice big cage.

"Parrots need a lot of space," said the saleswoman. "What type of parrot is it?"

"Seg something. I know. Segenal," Bunny said, with confidence.

"A Senegal. Hmmm," said the woman. "Yes, you need one about this size." She led Bunny down a row of cages, and then to a very large cage, although not the largest, and showed Bunny its bars. "These need to be close enough together so the parrot can't get its head stuck."

By the time Bunny got back out to the blazing hot parking lot of the PetParade, she had a box so enormous it could barely fit into the hotpinkmobile. But the strong young PetParade clerk the saleslady sent out to help her with the package did manage to get it into the trunk. He tied the trunk down with ropes while Bunny eyed his impressive muscles. *Too young*, Bunny's man-radar pinged.

Besides the enormous package in her trunk, the clerk loaded in Bunny's other finds: a big bag of parrot pellets ("Don't feed it seed—or not too much," cautioned the saleslady), a book on parrot care called "My First Parrot," a water bottle, and a shit-ton of parrot toys. "They need these so they won't get bored. Parrots are really smart. But they can chomp through their toys in a matter of days," the saleslady warned before Bunny left the store. "Parrots are not cheap pets. You didn't get your parrot from us. What did you pay for it, if you don't mind my asking?"

"I inherited it," Bunny lied.

"Oh," said the woman, her eyes sympathetic. "Parrots live so long. Frequently they outlive their owners."

"How long?" said Bunny.

"That parrot of yours. I'd say thirty, forty years. How old is it?"

"I'm not sure," Bunny admitted.

"Luckily, that kind of parrot shouldn't have much trouble bonding with you. An African Grey, now, one who was attached to its former owner—" The woman shook her head and shuddered. "In that case, I'd say you'd be in for a world of hurt. Not this bird." She looked doubtful. "Probably not."

Probably not, thought Bunny with a chill. Suppose it didn't like her, after all she was doing for it. Sazarac. Already she knew it didn't like Bingo, and the feeling was mutual.

It, she thought. *No. HE.* But of course she didn't know for certain. A DNA test cost upwards of a hundred bucks, though. And now that she didn't have her job. . .well, she just wasn't gonna pay, and that was that.

She sped back home, exceeding the speed limit. Just a bit. Hoping she wasn't gonna encounter Officer Baldridge on the way into town. If she had to encounter one, let it be Officer Gould. She could sweettalk Officer Gould out of a ticket. But she was worried about Sazarac. She sped up. Just a bit. By now, Sazarac must need more water, and Bunny doubted the lettuce she put into his carton would hold him long.

As she pulled into her driveway, she was stunned to see the big UPackWeDeliver truck pulled in too. And there he was. Finn. On her front porch, sitting just as bold as you please in her nice hanging double swing.

He stood when she triptrapped up to the front steps, taking care not to break off a stiletto on the gravel or turn an ankle.

He looked a bit sheepish. "Ma'am," he said.

"What're you doing here?" Bunny blurted out.

"Delivering a package."

Bunny's hand flew to her mouth. She'd forgotten all about it. Her package! The real package, the one she'd been expecting for the past week.

"I betcha you misdelivered the parrot instead of this one, and now you have to make it right. Well, you can't have Sazarac back. He's mine now, and I just spent a fortune in Elizabeth City on a big cage for him, and all the trimmings." She gave Finn a triumphant glare.

"No, ma'am," he said softly. "This is just another package for you. I'm, uh—" He coughed. "—gonna help you get it inside. It's a big package."

"The one I actually ordered," she said.

Bunny could hear Bingo on the other side of the front door. He was going crazy. "One sec," she told Finn. "Let me put Bingo up. He usually likes people, even strangers, but lately, with the parrot and all, I guess his routine has been disturbed. I'll be right back." She whisked into the house and stuck Bingo in the downstairs spare room, with a lot of comforting pets and a kiss on top of his soft, soft head.

When she came back to the front porch to sign for her package, Finn was looking past her to the hotpinkmobile with its tied-down trunk.

"That the cage? That's a big cage," he said. "Wow. That car is really pink."

"The saleslady said it was the type of cage I need," said Bunny, ignoring the remark about her car. "The saleslady knew all about—" Bunny paused to make sure she got it right—"Senegal parrots. She knew how wide apart the bars should be, and everything."

Finn was nodding his approval. "So. PetParade, not Fins 'n Feathers."

"Umm. Yes," said Bunny.

"Much more knowledgeable people in PetParade. Good choice."

"Glad you approve," said Bunny, her voice dry.

"I'll help you get the cage inside," he said.

"Bet that's against the manual."

He closed his eyes, briefly. "Yes," he said. "Where do you want it?"

Once they wrestled the cage and all the other gear up the porch steps, across the porch, and inside her house, Bunny sagged against the doorframe in dismay. "Where am I gonna put this thing?"

Finn looked around him. "Your front room looks nice. I'd say put the cage against a wall. You want your bird to feel safe. Like nobody's sneaking up on him."

Finn helped her move furniture out of the way and then unbox the cage and set it up against the far wall of her living room. It hulked back there on a tall practical-looking metal stand, looming out of place among Bunny's tasteful antiques.

Bunny ran water into the water bottle and affixed it to the cage. She put newspaper from the *Currituck Cove Nickel Shopper* on the cage bottom, and strewed parrot toys across it. Meanwhile, Finn was reading a page of directions and figuring out how to attach the perch. "Good perch," he approved. "Natural wood. Your parrot is going to chew on that thing. Some plastics are toxic. Parrots need to chew on things to keep their beaks healthy."

"Only one part left," said Bunny at last. "Sazarac himself."

She tiptoed into the kitchen. She'd had to put Sazarac's carton on the floor. She was too worried his frantic activity would toss his carton off the kitchen table with him in it. And so she'd had to be careful about keeping Bingo out of the kitchen.

Bingo was an unhappy dog.

She opened the carton and tried to grab Sazarac, who eluded her and snapped at her with his very vicious-looking beak.

"Let me," said Finn.

Bunny stood back and let him.

Finn tilted the carton carefully onto its side so he wasn't reaching down from above. He crouched at the opening, giving Bunny, behind him, quite the eyeful. He peered in, and moved his hand slowly into the carton's depths. After about an age of patient waiting, he drew his hand out with Sazarac perched on it.

"Yay!" said Bunny.

Sazarac flapped his wings.

"Ugh, suppose he flies away?" said Bunny. "Guess I better get his wings clipped."

"Please don't," said Finn. "Sure, some parrot owners do that. But it's terrible for the birds. And this guy isn't a baby. He has spent his whole life with all his wing power intact. Clipping a parrot's wings, that's so bad for them. You'll have an unhappy parrot if you do it. A screaming-all-the-time feather-plucker."

"We can't have that, can we, Sazarac?" said Bunny soothingly to the bird. She looked over at Finn. "But suppose he flies away?"

"Gotta keep the doors and windows closed. And, damn, you don't have ceiling fans, do you?"

"Yes, three, they have the nice vanes that look like palmetto leaves and they're so classy and beachy, and—"

"No," said Finn. "Turn them off. Right now."

Bunny bridled.

"Or prepare to scrape up a bundle of chopped up feathers from your very classy oriental rugs, and the beachy sisal one too."

Bunny rushed to turn the fans off. "This parrot is ruining my decor," she fumed.

When she returned, Finn was standing by the cage holding a big object in both hands.

Bunny boggled at it. "A watermelon?"

"Brought it over for you. Every parrot I've ever known loves watermelon."

"Thanks," said Bunny, faintly. "And thanks for helping me set up Sazarac's cage."

"Any time. Okay, this box I just delivered? Check before you sign. Make sure it's the right one this time."

"That wasn't my fault," Bunny grumped. "Someone sent me a parrot, and I have no idea why." She followed Finn out to the front porch.

He lifted the carton up as if it were nothing. "Where do you want it?"

She led him to the kitchen and pointed at the little café table.

"Check the box, please."

Bunny bent down to look at its label. She smiled. "This really is my package," she informed Finn.

When she looked up as she finished signing for it, she caught him smiling back at her. But maybe she imagined it. The smile disappeared. "I gotta go. I have a package to deliver." He whisked out the door.

A package to deliver. Bunny, gazing after his tight ass in the hot shorts, was very sure he did.

Putting a bird on it

AFTER FINN'S VISIT, when he'd been actually helpful and not judgy, or not much, Bunny began feeling a little more comfortable with parrot ownership. Sazarac, in his cage, was going to town on the watermelon chunks, and the toys, too, with all manner of fluttering and flapping and squawking. He looked pretty happy.

Bunny had peeked into the front room a couple of times. Her floor underneath the cage was getting messy. Bunny didn't do messy. She sighed and retreated to the kitchen. She hadn't gotten up the gumption to try to pick up the parrot again.

Bingo, after sniffing suspiciously at the cage, had left the living room to settle at Bunny's feet as she sat at the little café table. *Back in the kitchen again. Ahhh*. She heard him saying it, loud and clear, in Lab. She reached down to scratch his ears.

But her package! The one Finn had just delivered. The real package!

She set it down beside her on the floor and began extracting its contents, lining them up in a pleasing array on the café table. Her cosmetics supplies.

When she'd placed her order with the cosmetics supplies company, she'd decided she better start with something easy and basic. Lipstick.

In front of her she now lined up the adorable little tubs of wax that came with the kit, no less than seven different kinds. Beeswax. That's something she'd heard of. And carnauba and candelilla, maybe. Bunny squinted at the tiny labels. The others were a mystery to her.

She fingered the strange vials of chemicals with even stranger names. Two different types of vitamin E. Something called palmitate. Grapeseed oil, that one she recognized. She'd once tried a recipe that called for grapeseed oil. Or was that flaxseed?

But the colors! That part thrilled her most. Five or six different reds. A few blues. Some yellows.

She pulled out a thick brochure from the bottom of the carton. "Create Your Own Cosmetic Formulas: What You Need to Know." Her patented Bunny thousand-watt smile began to droop. After twenty minutes of reading, her eyes were crossing and her brain frying.

"This might have been a mistake, Bingo," she admitted. He nuzzled her. "I may not be up to this."

But she squared her shoulders. "I'm gonna try it," she declared. She decided she'd make three different colors of lipstick. She'd start out with the creamy ones. Nothing glitter, not at first. A true red, of course. A nice hot pink. Her signature color! "Of course I'll name it Hot Bunny Pink," she told Bingo. She looked over the color ingredients again, then back down at the directions. A kind of tawny, orangey red. She could get a color like that by mixing one of the reds with one of the yellows. Yeah. Perfect. The color of—

Bunny leaped up and dashed to the living room. She forced herself to approach Sazarac's cage slowly and calmly, although she wanted to bound toward it with all exuberance. She peered in. Yes! THAT tawny, orangey red.

Sazarac had a gray-blue head and a very fierce beak and eye. Most of the rest of him was a brilliant green. On his breast, the green feathers came to a point. "Sort of like he's wearing a bib,"

Bunny said to herself. And underneath his bright green wings and below that bright green bib? A beautiful tawny orangey red. In fact, that was the exact color of the cocktail in New Orleans she had so loved. A reminder of happier, more prosperous times.

So the name of this lipstick color she was just about to produce? A no-doubter. Sazarac.

"Okay, Sazarac," Bunny told him. "I'm beginning to like you. And also." Bunny had a brainstorm so massive she made a little fist-pump.

Sazarac screamed.

Bunny beamed at the bird. "You'll be my mascot. You'll be my logo. Sazarac, you're my lucky charm!"

By the end of the day, though, Bunny was ready to scream in frustration. Every time Sazarac screamed (often), she wanted to scream, too. She was about to have a full-on conniption fit. She had had to make herself many cups of coffee with her Keurig machine. Her favorite giant-sized mug, the white one with a big more or less Hot Bunny Pink lipstick imprint on it of giant lips, was by her side all day long.

The directions for making lipstick were so stuffed with difficult scientific terms, and warnings about which substances needed FDA and USDA approval, and directives about how and how not to mix the compounds, and discussions of spoilage, and how to do weights and measures with what sort of scales, and what kinds of utensils she would need, and what sort of fragrances, and what sort of packaging, and what sort of mailing service, that she was getting a headache.

The abrasive buzz of her doorbell didn't improve it.

Don't they make ring tones for these things? Bunny wondered as she padded to the door in bare feet to answer it. *Some kind of*

Parrot-head ringtone, she was thinking, as she flung open the front door.

In spite of the blasting AC, she was hot and flustered. Her mascara was in ruins. Her nail polish, fingers and toes both, was chipped and in need of renewal. She had barely combed her hair.

She like to die, the shame of it!

There stood Finn. Crisp in his shorts and his safari shirt. And—she gulped—young. Bunny herself was a young forty-two. Finn, though. She gulped again. Younger.

"I was thinking," he said with no preliminary, not seeming to notice how horrible she looked. "Yeah, see, I said to myself, give the lady a break, wouldja? That's tough, a creature like a parrot, with all its needs, and suddenly, no warning at all, it's on her doorstep. Not fair." He fixed Bunny with an earnest, fascinatingly green eye. "Not fair to you, and not to the animal. I could maybe help research how to send him back, or—was there any return address?"

I look like shit, she thought. "Don't you have packages to deliver?" she snapped.

"My shift is over. I was just about to head back to Elizabeth City, when—"

She stood on tiptoe to look past him. Leaning against the newel post of her front porch steps, a bike, the kind that meant business. And dangling by its straps from Finn's very muscular forearm, a helmet. Not the cute kind. The kind instead that made its wearer look like he was out of the pages of science fiction. Wasn't there a super-hero in the comics who sped around with something like that on his head? Speedo, maybe?

No. That wasn't his name. Speedo was a bathing suit brand. The kind that really defined a man's—

Breaking off the thought, she said instead, "You're gonna bike to Elizabeth City?" A part of her went, *No wonder you're so buff.*

He shrugged. "Not even thirty miles."

"In bad weather, I hope you take your car."

"No car."

"What are you gonna do once hurricane season hits?"

He squinted out over his shoulder to the ocean, just across the broad white-sand beach. "By then, I expect to be re-assigned back to Elizabeth City. It'll be okay. But about the parrot—"

"You can't have him back."

He tilted his head at her.

"Didn't you read the manual? That ever-loving manual of yours?" she goaded. "Live animal. I signed for him. I can't return him. He's mine."

"But you don't even like parrots. You know nothing about parrots."

"He's mine, and I'll learn. Just like I'll learn about these gol-darn chemicals." She muttered that last part to herself.

"What gol-darn chemicals?"

"Uh. I'm starting a business."

"With chemicals."

"Right."

"What kind of chemicals."

"Ye gods and little fishes. Was there a nosier delivery man in the history of delivery men, ever?"

"Ye what?" He stared at her, dumbfounded.

"Nothing. None of your beeswax." Suddenly she found herself bawling her eyes out, no transition at all, one moment mad as hell but perfectly normal, the next minute crazy as a shot-at rat, and Finn awkwardly patting her on the shoulder and sitting her down on the front porch steps. Just beyond the screen door, Bingo snuffled worriedly, whining a little.

"Beeswax," she wept. "So many different kinds of wax." *Are you nuts?* she asked herself, but she couldn't stop wailing. It was all her hopes and dreams, going up in the smoke of directives and regulations and technical requirements. And even more expensive equipment she needed but couldn't afford.

Bunny wept harder.

Plus, the weather was ungodly hot, muggy as the devil's armpit, and she looked like hell. Her hair hung in limp strands about her face.

"Lady, I'm not sure what's going on with you, but it'll be okay."

"No, it won't," she said, taking the tissue he offered and wiping her cheeks free of the streaks of mascara. "See, I thought—" She hiccupped.

"Take your time."

"I thought, now my company has folded and I'm out of a job, see, I thought, make your own. Right?"

"Um. Right." He leaned her head over on his shoulder and handed her another tissue. "Make your own what?"

"Cosmetics."

"Oh, god. With fragrances."

"Yes, although actually, that's the nice part. I'm thinking lavender. . ." She nestled her head against his shoulder. He felt really good. And speaking of fragrances, he smelled really good. Not perfumy. Like. . .she thought about it. Man-good. But she went on. "Tea tree. Vanilla."

"No," he said.

She sat bolt upright and threw his arm off indignantly. "Yes. Cosmetics need to smell good. The whole sensuous package."

"It's bad for parrots," he explained. He leaped to his feet. "Oh, god. I'll bet you're the type that— Any scented candles around? Aerosols? Room sprays? I'll bet you have room sprays," he accused. "You're just the type." He actually leaned over and sniffed her. "You smell good. Too good. That's bad." At her confusion, he added, "Bad for parrots. Especially the aerosols. Gotta get rid of those."

Bunny began bawling again.

Then it hit her. A bolt from the blue. A patented Bunny Dowdy Bolt From the Blue.

She sprang to her feet, dashing the tears from her eyes.

Finn flinched back.

She poked him hard in the chest. "That's it! Vegan cosmetics! Organic cosmetics. Or. . .something. A niche market, and it will be my niche! Nothing that's not natural. Bird friendly. Planet friendly. Wow."

She stared up at him, defiant and thrilled.

He looked back down at her. Man, he was a tall one. A little smile began playing at the corners of the full beautiful curve of his lips. He bent his mouth down close to hers, looked straight into the blue of her eyes from the green of his, and kissed her.

Bunny's lips parted all by themselves. She found she was standing on tiptoe and leaning into that kiss.

After a moment, she drew a breath. She stepped back a pace.

"I wasn't supposed to do that," he muttered, stepping back, too. "Sorry, ma'am. At least I'm off-duty," he muttered. "At least that."

"But you're still in uniform," Bunny pointed out.

He blushed crimson. He started buckling on his bike helmet. "You can call management to make a complaint," he told her tersely. "But don't spray anything perfumy around that bird. Don't spray anything at all around him. God. Not spray cleaners! Promise me none of that!" His face closed off. "But go ahead and file that complaint."

She put out a hand and touched him on the arm. "No complaints from here, Finn." She grinned. "You're a good kisser, and you don't find one of those on your front porch every day of the week. Besides, you just gave me the best idea ever."

He was righting his bike. "I should resign before it comes to complaints and firing and that."

"Finn. I'm not making a complaint."

He wasn't listening. "I don't exactly have the best track record."

"Don't resign," she said louder, from the top porch step.

He looked up at her, startled.

"I'm going to need a lot more advice," she said. "About Sazarac," she reminded, at his blank look. "And I don't want to have to drive all the way over to Elizabeth City to get it."

"I need this job," he said.

"So keep it. And come by tomorrow." She waved goodbye.

Finn went peddling off, and she got to stand out in the alley, shading her eyes to watch that nice tight ass speeding away from her. Why was it always heading away from her?

Surly

THE SAME TIME THE NEXT day, Bunny was ready for Finn. Hair brushed. Perfume gone. Fingers and toes freshly painted.

But Finn did not show. He didn't show the day after, either.

Aww, you are stupid, Bunny, she berated herself. She might be a good ten years older than Finn, and he probably went out with girls his own age. I mean, he was a good-looking guy, so why wouldn't he. Probably had some cute girlfriend over in Elizabeth City.

It's just that kiss, she told herself. *It got me off-kilter.* He probably kissed girls right and left and thought nothing of it. She looked in the mirror and adjusted the way her hair fell over her shoulders. Looked herself firmly in the eye. *Woman. Not girl. I'm no girl. That man could use a woman.*

Then she laughed at herself. What an airhead.

In a strange way, she felt better, though, because she had definitely made progress with the cosmetics. People always made the mistake of thinking she was some flighty bimbo. Then she showed them her business end. Then they were sorry they'd messed with Bunny Dowdy.

In the past few days, she had figured some things out, how she needed to start making the cosmetics, and she had put her good business sense to work, too.

She thrust Finn Mr. Hotpants firmly aside, put him into the box labeled "hot men, fun for a fling but don't take seriously," and wandered into the living room, Bingo padding alongside. They both went up to Sazarac's cage. He screamed at them.

"You're having a good time," she told him. "Glad somebody is." She thought about the man she had met in Paris, during her last big trip. That man was the real deal. The full package. But that life was over. Can't exactly sustain a romantic relationship with an entire ocean in between, and now, no more fancy, expensive trips. It was fun while it lasted, though.

Not fun, she thought a little sadly. Intense. Romantic. *They said it couldn't be done*, she whispered. *Break Bunny Dowdy's heart. They'd be wrong.*

The guy in New Orleans, now. Woooo-eee. What a nice distraction, once the Paris heartache was behind her.

"And now look at me. Jobless. A mess. No man." She grinned at Sazarac. "Just you and me now, buddy."

Bingo whined.

"And you, Bingo." She fondled his ears. "I'm your woman, you two."

She eased some parrot pellets into Sazarac's cage and took his water bottle off to refill it.

When she opened his cage door to reinstall it in its bracket, the miracle happened.

Sazarac stepped daintily up onto the back of her hand.

She drew him out of the cage, marveling. He took off. He was flying all over the house, zipping from room to room, and he looked positively joyous about it.

Bunny made herself coffee and slumped down on her sofa with the mug, pink with *Lipstick Goddess* emblazoned on it, to enjoy his antics. Flying all over the house. Pooping all over it too, looked like. Nice slogan, she thought, examining her mug. She filed it away for future consideration.

An hour later, she was getting a bit panicked. Sazarac was still relishing his freedom, and she couldn't entice him back to the cage. "What am I gonna do?" she asked Bingo.

Bingo didn't answer.

The doorbell buzzed.

Looking over her shoulder to make sure Sazarac wasn't in range to make a break for it out the door, she eased it open.

"Finn!"

"Peace offering," he said. Holding up another watermelon.

"Huh?"

"I'm sorry for stepping out of line. Thanks for not calling my manager. I was sure you would." He stood on her front porch, making his stiff little speech. "I deserved it."

She got a fistful of his tee shirt and pulled him into the house, quickly shutting the door behind him. "Fuck that," she said. "I've got real problems. He's out! And I can't get him to come back to his cage!"

"Okay," said Finn, knowing right away whom she meant by *he*. "Kitchen?"

"This way."

He stood at the kitchen counter slicing up the watermelon. Then, tempting chunk in hand, he was back in the front hall, making a little whistling sound.

Sazarac strafed them and flitted up the stairs to the second story.

"No windows open?" said Finn.

"No."

"Good. This is fine. Relax. Just a matter of time. Do you have some kind of longish stick?"

"Sec." Bunny whisked away. She reappeared with a piece of driftwood. "I had to dismantle my centerpiece, but here."

"Perfect," said Finn.

Finn stepped to the cage and put a chunk of watermelon on top of it. He put another inside.

Then he stood easy at the bottom of the stairs, the long piece of driftwood extended. He threw her an amused glance. "You're kind of a contradiction. 'Gol-darned' one minute, 'Fuck that' the next."

"You're not gonna swat him with that, are you?" said Bunny, hopping anxiously from foot to foot as he swung the stick around in a circle. She ducked.

"No." There was that delicious little curve of the lips again.

Sazarac zipped overhead back to the living room, to the kitchen, back to the living room, back up the stairs.

"Uh," said Bunny, looking aside at Finn, who was doing nothing at all now. She looked away. She was having a hard time not ogling.

Finn waited patiently, humming a little. A few minutes later, Sazarac swooped downstairs again, made a loop, and landed on the stick.

Very slowly, Finn moved with the perching Sazarac for the living room. They'd almost gotten there when Sazarac took off again.

"You gotta have patience, Bunny. It takes time, to get a bird like this to trust you." Finn waited with the stick outstretched.

Not too many minutes later, Sazarac came down for another landing, and this time Finn moved him deliberately to his cage. When Sazarac spotted the watermelon on top, he went for it, chowing down.

At Finn's offered hand, he stepped up, making little beak-snappings.

Finn moved him carefully to the cage door, where Saz could spot the second watermelon chunk inside.

As soon as he went for it, Finn closed the cage door. But softly.

"Don't make him feel like he's being put back in jail. His cage should be his cozy refuge."

"His cozy watermelon buffet," said Bunny.

"Exactly."

Bunny and Finn beamed at each other.

"Good birrrrrrd."

Bunny's head whipped around. "Did you hear that?"

"Saz, you rascal," said Finn, grinning. "You were just playing with us, weren't you? And now you've got what you wanted, and you're gonna be a good bird."

"Good birrrrrrd," agreed Sazarac.

"Look," said Bunny to Finn. "Let me make you dinner. It's 'way past dinnertime now."

Finn tilted his head dubiously. "Just when I got out of trouble with you, you're luring me back."

"You were never in trouble with me. C'mon. All I'm making's pasta."

He glanced at his watch. "Okay. It's summer, still enough light to get back to Elizabeth City safely."

"You're on that bike."

"Yeah. Hey, mind if I bring it inside? I don't want anyone stealing it. They probably won't, not around here, and I have a good lock, but—"

"Sure," said Bunny. "Bring it in and have a seat. I'll get the water boiling and fix a green salad."

As she hummed around her kitchen, getting out the romaine, starting the water, taking down the box of spaghetti and checking to make sure she had enough pasta sauce and parmesan, she was mentally boggling. This was the first time she'd seen Finn out of uniform, and oh man. She'd hardly been able to focus on the Sazarac problem, with him standing right there beside her.

Instead of the safari shorts, he had on tight lycra bike shorts. Instead of the safari shirt, a black tee with *Filthy Fifty* emblazoned over a guy peddling lickety-split somewhere on a bike. The tee showed off Finn's abs and how broad his shoulders were.

"Just about ready," she said, coming into the living room. He was leaning over the cage making encouraging noises at Sazarac.

"Okay." He turned to follow her into the kitchen. As they went through the hall, she paused to give his bike a once-over where it stood propped against the front door.

"That's an amazing machine," she said. It was gunmetal gray and shiny. It had a lot of gears and things on it. "And hey, you've named it! Pretty appropriately, if you don't mind my saying so."

He gave her a quizzical look before staring down at his bike. "Uh. That's not what I named it. That's the brand name," he said. Then, astounded, "You think I'm surly?"

"Well," she said, throwing up her hands. "When we first met, you have to admit—"

"You were about to let your parrot fry."

"No, I wasn't."

"Yes. You were."

They had a glaring stand-off in her front hall, until she heard the unmistakable hissing of water boiling over.

They ate the first couple or ten bites of dinner in a stony silence. They sat opposite each other at the café table in Bunny's kitchen. She had moved the entire clutter of chemicals and oils and waxes to her dining table in the dining room.

"Look, I'm sorry if I acted like a jerk, when we first met," he said at last. "I was just really worried about Saz."

"Okay," said Bunny.

"I was worried you didn't know enough about parrots not to hurt him."

"And you'd be right," said Bunny with a sigh. "It's so frustrating. I have tons of stuff to learn about parrots, tons of stuff to learn about cosmetics—and I'm a cosmetics goddess, I'll have you know."

"Yeah?"

Ignoring the amused gleam in his eye, she kept going. "Damn right. I'm the top-selling agent for the Adorable Me cosmetics line in all of Currituck County. Actually, in the whole southeastern region."

"Wow," he said. "So. What happened."

"Adorable Me went under." There was no way to sugar-coat it, so Bunny didn't try.

"And you can't find another cosmetics company to hire you?"

"You don't understand. It's a franchise kind of a thing. When they went under, I went under. My whole brand collapsed around me." She took a ragged breath. "I lost a lot of my savings." She gave him what she knew must be a crooked smile, but she'd be damned if she cried on him again. "I envy you. Here you are, working as a delivery guy, not a care in the world, and—"

"Not true."

"No?"

"No. Unfortunately, no. I had a good job in a big company, and then—then I lost it."

Something he'd said began to resonate with Bunny. Something after their kiss, something about not having a good track record. "You got fired," she said.

"Yep."

"For kissing someone," she guessed.

"Sort of." That smile again, tugging at the corners of his lips.

"Someone you were not supposed to kiss."

"My boss," he said. His shoulders sagged.

"Oh, man. Sexual misconduct."

"Uh. Well. . . "

"Well?"

"Look, it's like this," he said, kind of desperate, if you asked Bunny. "My boss and I fell for each other. Fell hard." His eyes got a faraway look. He cleared his throat. "That's not done. Somebody told HER boss. Now when something like that happens, somebody gets thrown under the bus, and somebody else usually comes out of it okay. Usually the higher-up comes out okay, and the underling gets it in the neck." Now he sounded definitely bitter.

"And you were the underling who got thrown under the bus. The one who got it in the neck." Very violent.

"That's the way I see it, anyhow."

"And now here you are, a delivery driver, and you're licking your wounds."

"That's just about the size of it," he said, taking another bite of pasta. "This is really good."

"Just bottled sauce."

"Umm, Bunny, I actually came over here with a—well, a thing I wanted to run by you. Now I feel like a dumbass even bringing it up."

She twirled her glass of red and took a sip.

He'd insisted on only water for himself. "I have to be out on the highway," he'd said.

"Just tell me," she said. "Let me be the judge of whether you're a dumbass."

"Okay, then. It's this. You don't have the space in this house to do what you need to do, and if you do try to do it in this space, you're gonna kill Saz."

"Ouch," said Bunny. "That sounds awful. So you're telling me give up my business idea or give up my parrot?" She was starting to get mad again.

"No. I thought of a solution."

"And?"

"It's kind of crazy."

"Spit it out, Finn."

"I have to move here," he said. "To the beach," he clarified.

"That's obvious," said Bunny, "but what does that have to do with me and my two problems?"

"Yeah, they're making me move over to the Currituck Cove office full time," he said bitterly. "And you were right. Hurricane season coming up, and I just have this bike for transportation."

"Hard duty," she said. "Having to live at the beach and all."

"Believe it or not, it's 'way more expensive over here than in Elizabeth City. This is a much smaller town, but it's the beach. Rentals here, they're all priced for tourists who can pay, and they are booked up for months, even into the fall."

"Huh. Okay. You're right. I had two friends move out of town recently, and they both were able to sell their houses for a lot more than they'd paid for them. Go on."

"So you know where the UPackWeDeliver is."

"That little office park out on the highway."

"You know how the Currituck Cove branch is in one of the storefronts facing the highway?"

"Right," said Bunny.

"But there are office spaces on the alley behind the complex. Not as desirable for a consumer business, but for light industrial? Just about perfect. One of them's for rent."

"Okay."

"Look, judging from what you've been telling me, you don't have a lot of extra cash to rent someplace, but you need to make your cosmetics far away from that poor bird." He gestured with his fork to the living room, where they could both hear Sazarac screaming and squawking. "And I sure don't have a lot of cash, either. What if we went in together and rented one of those places. You'd set up your operations there, and—"

"And what? You'd live there? I'll bet the leasing agent won't go for that. Look, I see what you're saying, Finn. Until last month, I rented a beautiful little office on the main drag. It was perfect. I sold my cosmetics out of that place, I had it decorated just the way I liked it." Bunny looked down at her plate. "Then I had to give it up. Just about killed me. So I do know about rents around here, and I do know the rent behind that complex would be pretty reasonable. But as for you—"

"Yeah, a bad idea, I guess." But he went on. "See, my thought is, I'd sort of be your silent partner. I'd give you my part of the rent, and you'd pay it and be the person who signed the lease. And I'd set up a cot back there, and a hot plate, I guess. There's a little rest room, and I'd—well, backed up to that office park is the Trucker's DLite, right? They have showers there. You'd never even know I was there. I'd be up and out of your way every morning before you got over there to work on your project, and I wouldn't go back there until you were gone again. I'd leave in the morning before business hours, so no one would see, and I'd come back after dark."

"Meanwhile, I'd be taking the risk that the rental agent would find out." Bunny raised an eyebrow. "Somebody actually living in light industrial space? Against all their rules. I'd be taking all the risk."

"That's true. Bad idea. I shouldn't have brought it up. I'm just kinda desperate, I guess."

"Here's another thing." Bunny pointed her fork at him. "Suppose you get another job, a job in your field, while we're trying our shady little experiment. Do I think you'll hang around being a delivery guy instead, just so you don't leave me in the lurch?"

"No," he said. "I thought that one through, and you're right. The second I get another decent job in my field, I'm out of this podunk town."

Bunny made herself ignore that slur on Currituck Cove.

Oblivious, Finn went on. "But I'll make an agreement with you to keep paying my part of the rent until the end of the lease. I think you can get six-month leases there. Not sure. Anyway, if I do get a job, I can afford to eat the rent."

"Geez, what do you do?"

"I'm a research chemist," he said. "I have feelers out. Friends looking around for me. I think I've got a good shot at a decent job. Not as good as the one I was booted out of, though."

"Coulda fooled me. I was sure you were a parrot smuggler."

"If chemistry doesn't work out, maybe I can switch fields," he said, giving her a wink.

I'm scared now

THE TROUBLE WAS. . . Bunny looked thoughtfully at Chet Martin, the rental agent, as she sat in his office at his round table in his office. Yeah, the trouble was, she knew these people. She and Chet had gone to kindergarten together. And now she was kinda telling Chet a lie.

Not telling him a lie. Just not telling him the whole truth.

But everyone in town knew Bunny. Everyone in town trusted her, and knew she had run her own business for years.

"This sounds like it could be a good thing for you, Bunny," Chet was saying. "Coffee?" He offered her a mug with his company logo stenciled on it. The mug was mud-brown. Bunny took it, thinking absently that she should hook Chet up with her friend Gina. Gina would design a logo that would look so much better than Chet's. And she would put it on a nice bright mug, lime green maybe.

Bunny took a cautious sip of coffee and set the mug down, resisting the temptation to spit it out. "Oh, start-ups, you know. My little business may fold."

"Well, you could save on a year's lease, but I see why you'd want the six-month," he said easily. "You can test out the idea without a whole lot of risk."

"That's my thought, Chet. Now, I'll be making cosmetics back there. Anything to say I can't? Chemicals and stuff. Would that be a problem for you?"

"No, it's fine," said Chet. "I mean, Florella Spiritsong is making soap two doors down from you. Those little soaps with all the herbs in them."

He and Bunny rolled their eyes. Florella Spiritsong was one of the people in their high school graduating class, Brenda Hutchinson. She'd gone hippy and changed her name and started making and selling the hippy-dippy little soaps.

Bunny stirred uneasily, remembering her days of going by a Frenchified version of her own name, Bérénice, to sell the high-end lines of Adorable Me more effectively. Adorée and Mélisande, they were called. Fine high-end personal products.

Unfortunately, although Bunny had done well selling them, most of the other Adorable Me reps had floundered.

Problem was, these fancy products weren't Adorable Me's core business.

Adorable Me had started out recruiting a fleet of reps who would bring their cases into a woman's home and sell to her and her friends right there on the woman's kitchen table. Party-plan stuff.

Then Adorable Me had gone upscale. It had grown too fast, too soon, and then it had gone under.

Pretty judgy of her to sneer at Brenda/Florella, Bunny realized, thinking of her Bérénice persona.

It made her a little sad, too. Bérénice was the one her Paris hottie Etienne had fallen for, not the actual Bunny. Now Etienne was gone, and so was Bérénice.

Bunny smiled at Chet. "Where do I sign?"

Chet plunked the lease down on the table, Bunny signed, and then she wrote a check for the deposit, near-wiping out her bank account.

Late that afternoon, Finn was over to help load up the hot-pinkmobile with all Bunny's chemicals and waxes and cosmetic-making gear.

"This will keep Saz much safer," he told her.

"This is nuts, is what it is," Bunny muttered under her breath. "What am I thinking? What am I doing?"

Finn heard, though.

He stuffed a lot of Bunny's cosmetics-makings into her trunk and then he turned to her. "Look, I'll probably get a job soon. Then I'll pay what I owe you up front for the rest of the lease, and you can have a dirt-cheap lease for six months. Long enough to let you know whether you really do want to pursue this thing."

"I got a D in high school chemistry," Bunny said gloomily. "Now I've become a chemist."

"Not exactly," said Finn, with that little quirk to the corner of his lips.

"Just call me Walter White," she gloomed.

He shook his head. "Jesse Pinkman."

"Yeah. Right. You're right. As always."

"Bunny. Don't worry. Pretty soon YOU will be the one who knocks."

"Yeah!" said Bunny, brightening immediately. "I'm gonna get one of those hats."

Finn laughed out loud at her. "A fellow *Breaking Bad* fan," he said.

"Who knew we'd have anything in common," said Bunny.

"Who knew such a prissy lady would watch such a violent show."

Bunny's mouth sagged open. *Prissy.*

"Oh, now, Bunny. I didn't mean that the way it sounded."

"Yes, you did." She whirled on him, hands on hips. "You wanna know something, Mr. Finn Johansen?" At least she knew his last name now. "People always do that. You're not the first."

"Do what?"

"Underestimate me. Then later they're sorry."

"I believe you," said Finn, throwing up his hands. "I'm scared now."

"Oh, get in the car," she said. She pulled out of the alley and drove, just a bit too fast, out to the highway. She swung around in back of the UPackWeDeliver.

It was dark by then.

By the light of streetlamps in the back parking lot, Bunny fished for her new set of keys and let them both into the long shadowy room that would become her cosmetics factory.

"If anyone sees us back here, there's an easy fix," she told Finn. "We'll just say I hired you for a few hours to help me move all this stuff."

At one end of the long room was a pretty large storage closet and a bathroom. No shower, though.

"You really think it will work, going over to the truck stop for showers? I thought only truckers got to use those."

"Nope," said Finn. "As I've come to know during this nomadic period of my life, anyone can pay for a shower at one of these places. They're usually pretty clean. Good idea to bring your own soap and shampoo rather than use the stuff in the truckstop dispensers, though. Good idea to bring flip-flops. I like to bring my own towel, too."

"Aren't the charges gonna mount up?"

"I'll manage," said Finn. "I've done the math. Now that my rent's so cheap, I'll just think of the shower charges as part of the rent I'm paying."

He went out to the parking lot to haul in a folding cot he'd be using. He stored it against the wall. Then he and Bunny positioned a long table in front of it, so anyone casually glancing around wouldn't get a good look at it and wonder what Bunny was doing with it in there.

They set up a cheap chest of drawers from Goodwill in the storage room, for Finn's clothing—mostly UPackWeDeliver uniforms with UPWD embroidered on the pockets, and his array of bike shorts and tees. And his underwear.

"Tighty-whiteys," said Bunny, wrinkling her nose.

"You're criticizing my underwear now?"

She turned aside without answering, to set up his two-burner electric stovetop on a table at the far other side of the room, and her Keurig machine, and a toaster oven, with one of those little dorm-sized refrigerators underneath. She'd helped him haul that over from his tiny Elizabeth City apartment.

Then she started unboxing her cosmetics supplies and arranging them down the two long tables that dominated the room. Finn brought in a miscellany of folding chairs Bunny had found in her basement.

"Now for my office," Bunny said. While Finn assembled a folding partition, Bunny shoved a small rolling desk and rolling organizer into place, and a printer stand. She'd bring her laptop back and forth from home, and she'd gotten a cheapo inkjet printer and a label printer for the new industrial digs.

These they put right beside the door.

"All done," said Bunny brightly. They went off for Chinese take-out, "My treat," said Bunny, and then Bunny dropped Finn at the Piggly Wiggly just down the highway from the office park.

She handed him his own set of keys as he got out of the car.

"This is probably a big mistake," she told him, as he leaned over to take the keys.

"Probably. But listen, I've got leads on three jobs, and one of them starts pretty soon. It's in Minnesota," he added.

"Your home state."

They'd already established that Finn was indeed a Yankee, although Finn had objected to the label.

"That's New Englanders," he'd said. "I'm from the Upper Midwest."

Bunny hadn't argued.

Yankee, she thought, setting her jaw. "Just saying the word 'Minnesota' makes me feel cold. Brrr."

"This steamy climate? Just saying 'Currituck Cove' makes me hot," he countered.

Bunny, pulling away to drive home, glancing back at Finn where he stood under the lighting of the Chinese place in the biker shorts that molded to his body and revealed the outline of his junk for all to see, had to agree with that.

Lipstick Goddess

"ACK!" FINN SAT BOLT upright on his cot, his hair sticking up. "What time is it?"

"8 a.m." Bunny said. "So much for being gone before I get over here, and before business hours."

"Overslept. Really sorry." He sprinted for the bathroom, just a flash of tighty-whiteys. She heard toothbrushing and gargling going on in there.

She headed for the other end of the long room to fire up the Keurig.

When he came out all safari-suited up, she handed him a cup.

"I'm late for work."

"Too bad. Breathe. Drink a cup of coffee." She scrutinized him over the rim of her own mug, the one with *Bite Me!* stenciled on it in red.

He took the *It's Raining Men!* mug she was holding out, a souvenir from last year's karaoke night at the town singles club. Then he reached past her to stick a toaster pastry into the toaster oven.

"Really? Toaster pastries. They taste like cardboard."

"If you get the generic, a buck seventy-eight for a box of twelve at WalMart." He gulped the coffee.

"I make myself bacon and eggs every morning."

He boggled at her. "Not—" he hesitated. "Not in a non-stick pan, though."

"Yes, in a non-stick pan."

"Aargh. Bunny. Those things give off fumes. And that's—"

Bunny put her own coffee cup down carefully. "Let me guess. Bad for parrots."

"Yes, very bad for parrots. Gotta be stainless steel." He fixed his eyes earnestly on hers.

Bunny laughed a little. "Hey, I'll make a bargain with you. I'll buy a stainless-steel frying pan if you buy some sexier underwear."

"Had some. Threw it away."

"You threw it away?"

His face darkened. "SHE got it for me."

Ha, Bunny thought. That boss of his, the one who had thrown him under the bus. The one who had come out on top while he got it in the neck.

He put his coffee cup down on the little table that served as the Keurig machine's shrine. He cracked the exit from the Lipstick Lab open. "Coast is clear. Sorry for overstaying this morning. Lot on my mind, couldn't sleep last night." He eased out into the parking lot. "Tighty-whiteys, ten bucks and change for a six-pack at WalMart," he said over his shoulder.

Leaving Bunny the whole morning to think about the six-pack underneath the tan UPWD shirt.

But she did manage to get some work done. Now she had concocted three little sample tubs of lipstick. One was a beautiful bold red. She'd have to decide what to call that. And the Hot Bunny Pink. And the Sazarac.

Except it was all kind of runny. At least it smelled good. In this parrot-free environment, she could experiment with fragrance to her heart's content.

She smeared some of the Hot Bunny Pink on her lips. It did smell good. Camelias. Organic camelias. She could say that much.

A nice pink fragrance. Problem was, the stuff didn't feel like lip-stick. It didn't even feel like lip gel. It sort of dripped.

By the end of the day, she was pretty frustrated. She hadn't solved her drippage problem.

She headed home early to walk Bingo and feed him, and to feed Saz. But she carefully wiped all the mouth goo off first, and washed her face.

A long walk on the beach with a black lab who keeps frolicking off into the surf was just the thing.

When she got back, Bunny was a lot more relaxed. Several days ago, she'd also ordered more parrot toys, and there they were, in a box left on her front porch. She groaned. She had missed Finn. He must have been the one who delivered them. He seemed to be the UPWD's only delivery driver.

Bunny peered into Saz's cage. He had viciously demolished all the first parrot toys. Well, the saleswoman at the PetParade had warned her he would.

She scooped fragments of defunct parrot toys from the bottom of the cage and dumped new ones in.

"Good birrrrrrrd," commented Saz.

"Wish I could let you out, Saz," she told him. "But I have had a Bunny brainstorm, and I need to leave again."

Not a patented Bunny Bolt From the Blue. It was too modest for that. But a pretty good idea.

It was after working hours but still light when she headed back up the highway, grabbing Chinese take-out on the way.

At the door to The Lipstick Goddess, she hesitated. Then she knocked.

Nothing.

Oh, geez. She needed to text Finn. Otherwise he'd pretend he wasn't in there.

After her text, he cracked the door and looked out.

She dangled the take-out bag at him.

He let her in.

"I know I'm encroaching on your time and all," she began.

"As if I didn't encroach on yours this morning," he said. "Umm." He looked at her, a little shyly, she thought. "I got you something. Here." He handed her a small bag.

With a squeal, she pulled out the object it contained: a mug with Walter White on it in his Heisenberg hat. "You know how to make a girl feel good!"

Finn actually blushed.

"I came over to pick your brain," she told him. "Here's some Chinese to go with that."

"Chinese food and brains. I'm really working up an appetite."

They spread paper towels out on an end of the long table "where I don't think any poisonous stuff has been," Bunny said.

Then they ate from the little cartons of Moo Goo Gai Pan and Beef With Broccoli, washing it down with a Diet Cheerwine for Bunny, plain water for Finn.

"Bet that stuff's bad for you," said Finn, eyeing Bunny's Diet Cheerwine.

"Don't tell me it's bad for parrots."

His lips quirked up. "No, I figure parrots are too smart to touch that stuff. What is it, anyway, wine?"

"No, just cherry soda."

"Diet cherry soda. Not bad for parrots, but you? One day you will glow in the dark, Bunny Dowdy. Okay, what do you want to pick my brain about?"

"I spent all day trying to make lipstick, and just look at it."

She found the little tubs and thrust them under Finn's nose.

"They smell nice," he said cautiously.

"Yeah, but the consistency. It's all wrong. I thought maybe you could give me some tips. I'm following all the directions in the brochure, but I've gotta be doing something wrong."

Finn launched into a long explanation of what that could be, liberally peppering it with terms she didn't understand.

Finally he stopped and stared at her. "This can get a little complicated," he said.

"You're saying I'm not smart enough to figure it out."

"No. Absolutely not. Just that this kit you bought makes it all sound easy, and it's not that easy."

"I guess I have to try harder," she said quietly.

"Look. Bunny. You're doing me a huge favor. Why don't I help you out?"

"You'd do that?"

"Hey, I have almost as big a stake in Cosmetics Goddess's success as you do."

Now it was her turn to grin. "Too many esses in that name. Makes it hard to say. Thought I'd call it Lipstick Goddess."

"See? You know marketing. I know chemistry. Let me give it a shot."

"Okay. But first, I have a suggestion."

"What's that?"

"Uh. This morning, you didn't have time to get over to the Truckers' DLite, did you? And now—"

"Are you trying to tell me with typical Southern Gal indirectness that I have B.O.? I'm sure I do, after no shower and a long day delivering in the heat."

"So here's my suggestion. I know you have it all worked out, the trucker shower, the laundromat down the street, but suppose you gather up all the sweaty clothes, plus your sweaty bod, and come over to my house for a shower?" When he hesitated, she said, "Saz will be happy to see you. Hell, even Bingo. He has gotten used to you."

Back at her house, she grabbed all his dirty laundry and headed to the basement washer with it.

When she came upstairs, she tossed him something red. He caught it. "What's this?"

"Bathing suit. I always have them lying around. You live at the beach, people visit. Then they leave their bathing suits by mistake." She nodded at the skimpy red number she'd handed him. "It's clean. I throw them in the laundry. Okay, I'm going to put my own suit on, and then let's hit the beach before it gets dark. Bingo will love it, and when we get back, showers."

She didn't say "a shower," did she? Of course not. He might misunderstand. She said "showers."

When they floundered back out of the surf and onto the beach, they were both laughing and relaxed. The summer sun was just setting.

"Here I've been working at the beach for over a month, and this is the first time I've actually been to the beach, you know?" His eyes sparkled.

She couldn't help checking him out, hoping she wasn't being too obvious. Saltwater was streaming down his broad chest with its mat of black hair, and the red bathing suit was maybe a delightful size too small. Then she realized. He himself wasn't worried about being obvious at all. He was so checking her out. He so was.

"Wow," he said. "You look pretty great in that bikini. Not every woman can wear that kind and look good doing it."

"Thank you," she said, with a demure smile.

He leaned over to her seriously. "You know," he said. "You look just great without any makeup. You know that, right, Lipstick Goddess?"

"Oh," she waved a dismissive hand. "When we women get a little older, we need a little—"

"No, you don't. You don't need a thing."

So then they ended up kissing again, and when Bunny pressed her wet sandy body against his wet sandy body, she let herself think, "a shower." Not "showers." Because this man wanted her. She could feel exactly how much.

A better idea

ONCE BUNNY AND FINN had hosed Bingo off and hosed the sand off their own feet, Bunny led Finn upstairs to her own bathroom and showed him where the towels were. She turned to leave.

He grabbed her by the hand and pulled her gently back to him. He bent his face down to hers and kissed her again, a lot more thoroughly, this time.

Deliciously, as if he were eating a particularly juicy peach.

She threw her arms about his neck to pull him down closer to her and press their bodies more closely together. She wanted to feel that long hard shape against her again, the sign of how much he wanted her. It was getting longer and harder.

With one hand, he cupped her chin. With the other—

She shivered in anticipation.

He undid the strings holding the top of her bikini in place. Then he buried his face between her breasts, groaning.

She took his hands in hers and led him out of the bathroom and down the short hall to her bedroom, bumping the door open with a hip.

They fell together onto Bunny's bed. Finn swatted a multitude of little cushions and decorative pillows off it. He rolled over on top of Bunny, taking first her right breast and then her left into his mouth. Bunny found herself making hungry squeaky noises.

He rose on his elbows above her, and she could feel his hard member nudging at her bikini bottom.

His hair flopped into his face. His breath was coming hard. "But I don't have—" he began.

She groped for the drawer pull of her bedside table, found it, and extracted a little foil package. "Looking for one of these?"

He blew out a laugh.

"I'm a big girl, Finn, and I know what I want."

"You want this?"

"I want you," she said.

He skinned the red bathing suit off himself. With trembling fingers, he pulled apart the foil and rolled the condom down over his erection.

Bunny propped herself up to watch. "I want THAT," she said, wriggling out of her bikini bottom.

"And that wants this," said Finn, his member insisting at the lips of her entrance. "Wait," he said.

He slid down the bed until he could bury his face in her crotch, kissing her down-there lady-lips and murmuring her name.

Bunny gasped. Her hips arched to him. She ran her hands into his hair, urging him closer, and moaned. She tugged at him to pull him higher, but he didn't budge.

"Tell me how much you want me," he said hoarsely, his voice muffled.

"I do. I want you. Finn. I do."

"How much."

"More," she gurgled.

"Like this?" The man was good with a tongue, she'd give him that.

"Like that," she panted.

"How much."

"I want you inside me."

"Not yet. Not until you tell me you're gonna explode."

"I'm gonna explode, Finn."

"I want you to explode more."

"Finn!" she about screamed.

He rose and carefully eased his length into her, filling her up. He thrust. Then, carried away, he pounded at her, and she was screeching and holding on for dear life. When she thought she couldn't stand it one more minute, she saw stars, and gasped out—something, she wasn't sure what, everything went white and miraculous, like swooping over the top of the ferris wheel at the county fair, or the teakettle coming to a shrieking boil. Then he was gasping too, crying out and coming hard inside her.

He collapsed down on top of her.

Such a lovely weight.

She stared up at the ceiling, her breath slowing, her smile growing.

"God, Bunny."

"Don't swear," she whispered.

"You are." He took a deep ragged breath in. "So delicious."

"Don't move. Don't leave. I want you right here. I have to hold you."

"I want to be right here. I want you to hold me," he said.

They might have dozed a bit. After a little while, he rolled off her and they lay smiling together. He reached out a hand and brushed the hair out of her eyes. "That was incredibly good," he said. "You liked it, right?" He turned to her suddenly, his green eyes anxious.

"Liked it? Lordy, Finn. You about transported me to Mars."

Looked like to both of them the Mars rocket was ready for another take-off.

"Okay," he groaned at last. "Shower." After his shower, he came in to sit on the side of her bed, one of her towels wrapped around his torso. He ran his hand up and down her arm gently, slowly, as if she were a precious and breakable object. "I think all my clothes are in your washing machine."

"I'll get up in a minute and put them in the dryer."

"No, tell me where. I can do it, and you won't have to move." He leaned down and kissed her lightly on the lips.

After a little while he was back. "I give it forty minutes, maybe."

"I have a better idea," said Bunny. She grabbed at the towel and whisked it away from him. "Aha!" she said triumphantly.

Already he had a hard-on. Another one.

She eyed it, hungry for him all over again. "Just come back to bed, Finn."

And so he did.

Early the next morning, her eyes blinked open. "Crap," she said.

He was already safari-suited-up. "Damn." He ran a hand over his chin. "I need to shave. Guess I'll go for the scruffy look today."

"I like the scruffy look. Right now I'm imagining what that scratchy face would do if you ran it up my thigh." She made her lips into a little pout. "No morning sex."

"I wish," he said. "But I can't be late to work two days in a row."

"How are you gonna get back there? I drove us in the hot-pinkmobile last night. Your bike's still at the Lipstick Lab. You're my prisoner."

"That's harsh," he said, grinning.

"Aww, I'll drive you back. Ten minutes?"

"Okay."

She gave herself a quickie shower, wishing he were in there with her. Remembering her idea of the night before, shower sex. It had never happened.

Mournfully, she came back to the bedroom to put on a pair of lacy undies and shorts and a lacy bra, and a tee that showed her figure off, while he sat on the side of the bed watching and making appreciative noises. "I like those frilly pink little. . .whatever they are."

She looked over at him, an eyebrow arched. "I suppose you are fully armored in the tighty whiteys."

"Nope." He grinned again. "Going commando today."

"No fair!" she screeched. "You're gonna leave me all hot and bothered, thinking about that."

"Tell me about it. Let me hobble bow-legged out to your car, ma'am."

Bunny gave Bingo a quickie walk, while Finn performed quickie Saz care.

"Everything," Bunny grumped, leading the way to her car, "except an actual quickie."

Finn looked the hotpinkmobile over, shaking his head. "Every time I see this thing, I'm amazed all over again."

"It was a prize. For selling the most cosmetics in my division," she added.

"That explains it. I guess. Couldn't you have made them give you a nice green one, or a blue one, or—"

"How dare you insult my car? The hotpinkmobile is the world's best car. Only the best car care for her. See? That's how you can tell I'll turn out to be a good parrot parent, even though I don't know beans about parrots. Look how good I am to Bingo. Look how good I am to this car."

"She's ten years old if she's a day," said Finn, sliding into the passenger side, eyeballing the *Have Mug Will Travel* number in the cupholder. "But I can see it for myself." He patted the upholstery. "In mint condition. And Bunny." He looked sidelong at her, shaking his head. "This car is you. This is your color."

"Was there ever the shadow of a doubt about that?" Bunny pulled out of the driveway and headed for the UPWD.

Not the usual fling

BUNNY AND HER TWO BEST friends were having lunch at The Mermaid, their favorite lunch place ever.

"Sure is good to see you back here, Gina," said their waitress, Paula, as she waited on the three of them. "I've seen Fran from time to time." She was pouring iced teas for all of them, and she had remembered that Gina, one of Bunny's two friends, didn't like The Elixir of the South. Sweet tea.

"Yeah, Fran didn't move far," Bunny agreed.

"Elizabeth City's practically next door," said Fran.

"Wow, it's great to be back," said Gina, smiling at Paula, her eyes roving in delight over all the tacky décor, the smirking ship's figurehead mermaid hanging over the bar, the netting, the cork floats. The worn-out linoleum of the floor. "I'll have the chicken salad with walnuts."

Paula grinned. Bunny and Fran grinned with her. Gina always got the same thing.

"No sweet tea for you, either, Miss Bunny," said Paula, pouring Bunny's and handing her a little packet of artificial sweetener.

"That stuff's bad for you, Bunny," said Fran, eying the artificial sweetener.

"I'll take my chances. A friend of mine claims I'm gonna start glowing in the dark."

"A friend." Gina leaned across the table from her side of the booth. "Hmm. Let me imagine what kind of friend."

"Oh, y'all," said Bunny, rolling her eyes.

"You should settle down, Bunny, like your two settled-down married friends," said Fran.

"Never," said Bunny. She changed the subject. "Did you bring your suit, Gina?"

"Of course I brought my suit. And how's Bingo, my favorite pooch? Or, well. . .my second-favorite."

"Don't go telling Bingo that. He'll get jealous."

Over coffee in The Mermaid's signature mugs with the fish handles, Gina handed her phone over so the other two could admire Bongo, one of Bingo's pups, now Gina's dog. And also admire Doug, her handsome husband.

Then it was Fran's turn for the family photos.

"But Gina," said Bunny. "Bingo has a friend now. Wait'll you meet him."

"You got a puppy!"

"Nope. A parrot."

The other two gave her the side eye like maybe she was two tacos short of a combination plate.

"Didn't figure you for the parrot type, Bunny," said Fran.

"It was sort of an accident. But now there are three of us. Me, and my two guys. Bingo and Sazarac." Bunny flashed her own family pics. Her, rocking her bikini. Bingo looking soulfully into the camera. Saz screaming into it.

"And who is that?" said Gina.

"Who's what?" said Bunny, trying for an innocent look.

"That's a definite man-hand, with your parrot perched on it."

"My friend."

"Who must be the one who took the bikini shot," Fran guessed.

"Aww, Bunny. I'm glad. Because after Paris. . ." Gina began.

"Yeah." Bunny felt gloomy. "Paris. That was a blow. But it was so not me. I don't do serious. I don't do heartache."

The other two laughed and rolled their eyes.

"So this new guy isn't serious," said Gina.

"Serious? What're you talking about? I'm never serious."

"Almost never," said Gina gently.

"The Paris thing. I'm so over that. Nope. Right now I'm just having fun. I love men. And I love men for one reason." She arched a brow at their expressions. "Fun."

"Are we going to meet this new fun guy?" said Gina.

"I doubt it. He's busy. He is a delivery man."

Fran and Gina giggled at Bunny. "Even the delivery men of Currituck Cove aren't safe from you, Bunny," said Fran.

Bunny giggled too.

But she felt a kind of nagging worry. She'd told Finn she wouldn't be at the Lipstick Lab for four whole days. A friend visiting.

"So you'll have the Lab all to yourself," she'd said. Then she had rounded on him. "Think I'm a lightweight, don't you. Think this is just some bimbo's hobby. I work on it a while, then I'm off having fun in the sun."

"I don't think that, Bunny," Finn said. "While you're gone, I'll try to put in some hours with the formulas. Pull my weight around here. Don't worry. Have fun with your friend." His eyes had darkened.

The way he said that—. Bunny had thought it over as she had driven to The Mermaid.

She was still thinking about it as she slid into the three friends' usual booth, hugs all around. Finn thought she had a man friend coming to visit her. Well, let him think it. It would be good for him.

Let him know where he stood. Let both of them know, him and herself both. This thing with Finn, it was just fun. Just a summer fling. He'd be out of there and back to Idaho or Montana or wherever he was from, and Bunny would zip along to the next fun time.

Minnesota, she whispered to herself. Her heart gave a little wrench.

"What about Minnesota?" Fran said.

"Oh, did I say that out loud? Nothing," said Bunny.

Later, when Fran had driven away back to Elizabeth City, Gina followed the hotpinkmobile to Bunny's house on the beach.

"My goodness, Bunny," she said. "This is different."

Bunny's house had morphed from something out of *Southern Living* into Parrot Heaven.

Bunny didn't defend herself. "Parrots are very needy creatures. They need everything just so. Oh, by the way, you didn't bring any kind of perfumy spray with you, did you?"

"No," said Gina. "You know me, Bunny. You and Fran had to practically tie me down to give me a makeover that one time."

"You look great, Gina. How's Doug?"

"He's fine. He's off at some charity golf thing. Great timing, because I was pining away for the beach, even though the mountains are beautiful."

"You should have brought Bongo."

"What a crowd that would have been. You, me, Bingo, Bongo, and Saz. No, I left Bongo with his favorite dog-sitter. He's so cute, though. I'll miss him. Maybe more than Doug." Gina's eyes sparkled mischievously.

"Not a chance," said Bunny. "You're so in love." She sighed.

Gina touched Bunny lightly on the arm. "You should try it. Falling in love."

"I did. Remember? Didn't go too well."

Then they were off on other topics, and out on the beach sunbathing, and in the surf, and cooking scrumptious dinners together.

It wasn't all fun and frivolity. Bunny spilled the gory details about trying to start her own cosmetics company. Gina nodded. She knew. She'd started her own jewelry business. They talked through all the pitfalls.

"You should game this out with Fran, too," said Gina.

Fran had retired from banking, but Bunny knew Gina was right. Why hadn't she talked it over with Fran? Bunny felt uneasily it might have something to do with Finn, with not really wanting her friends to know about Finn. But why? The thing with Finn was just a fling, and her friends knew very well how much she enjoyed one of those. It might not be their thing, the carefree fling, but for Bunny, it was an art form, and her friends loved her just the same, even though it wasn't their art form.

The time flew past.

"I hate it that you're leaving so soon," Bunny said on their last morning together as they ate bacon and eggs in Bunny's kitchen. Bunny stood scraping the eggy bits off her stainless-steel frying pan while Gina went off to the spare room for last-minute packing.

Bunny bustled in with laundry straight from the dryer. She stopped short in the doorway.

Gina was sitting on the spare-room bed, grinning, twirling a pair of tighty-whities around one finger. "Look what I found under the bed."

"Oh—" Bunny felt herself blushing.

"Bunny, this isn't your usual fling. Can't fool me, girlfriend. I can tell."

"Finn's kinda different."

"Finn!" screamed Gina. "His name is Finn?"

"Yeah. Look, Gina. It's nothing serious. He's a lot younger than me, for one."

"Who cares about that?"

"Whatever," said Bunny. "I'm having a lot of fun. Not thinking past that. Not gonna over-think it. It's just the summer, you know. Summer at the beach."

"He's just here for the summer?"

"Yes. Probably. Maybe."

"Not a summer resident, though. A delivery man, you said."

"Yep."

"Wow, things have changed. Can't fool me, Bunny Dowdy. This isn't your usual fling." Gina it said again, with emphasis. "Your house is not your usual house, not any more. I can't imagine anything powerful enough to cause a change like that. Except maybe one thing."

"Good birrrrrrd," came Sazarac's voice from the living room.

"I have a parrot to think about now," said Bunny.

"Responsibilities," said her friend, nodding seriously. Trying to hide the little smile that crept across her face.

Drawing a line

FINN PICKED AN UNCLUTTERED space on one of the long tables in the Lipstick Lab and unfolded the glossy brochure.

Bunny read over his shoulder.

It was the Fourth of July holiday, and Finn got one extra day off. "I may as well spend it working on your formulas," he told her.

"No girlfriend back in Elizabeth City to see?" said Bunny, keeping her tone light. From time to time, they went off together at the end of the workday to have beach fun and more fun later, in bed. But everything was about keeping it light.

"Nope. No more girlfriends for me," he answered in the same playful tone. But his eyes darkened, in that way they had. Bunny had learned the signs. "Too dangerous."

Bunny nodded. "Under the bus. In the neck. So okay, what's this?" She tapped the brochure with a finger.

"It's a conference I should go to."

"Pricey," Bunny commented.

"Yeah, but I can make job connections there. If I'm lucky, I'll even have an interview or two lined up at the conference center."

"I don't understand."

"The interviewers for big companies go to these conferences. If you've applied for one of their jobs and you make the first cut, they'll interview you at the conference. Then later maybe invite you out to their site."

"So you're a really good chemist?"

"I think so. What do you think, Ms. Bunny Dowdy?" He reached over and took one of the little lipstick tubs between thumb and forefinger. "Try this."

It was a tub of the Hot Bunny Pink. She sniffed in the wonderful fragrance of camelias. Then she dipped her finger in. It felt exactly right. She took the little tub into the tiny bathroom and looked in the mirror while she smoothed some of it over her lips. The consistency was exactly right. It looked exactly right!

She emerged beaming. "Perfect, Finn!"

"Don't you have to put it in a kind of tube thing?"

"I could. Or I could sell it in these adorbs little tubs."

He grinned at her. "There you are, rocking your color."

She preened. "My signature color."

"I want to kiss it off you," he growled. "But." He sighed. "I have to get my conference registration in before the deadline. Luckily, I just got paid."

"It's not too far away, either. Raleigh."

"Yeah."

"Finn. I have an idea. Let me drive you. How were you planning to get there, anyway?"

"I'll think of something. I can't let you drive me there."

"Why not? I love Raleigh. I can do some shopping there. We can get a nice hotel room. Hotel king-size bed, with all the little soaps and lotions in the bathroom!"

"I can't afford that."

"I'll pay." She tapped the table with her fingertips. "Hmm. Wonder if Brenda has thought of placing her soaps in hotels. I should mention it."

Finn was focused on the hotel and what it would cost. "If I let you pay—No. I can't let you. Sometimes, I feel like a kept man around you, Bunny." He took a lot of showers at her place. Or rather, they did. Together. It was heaven.

"You pay your part of the rent. Look, I'll let you pay half the hotel room."

"I was gonna stay someplace really cheap."

"Pay half what that would be, then."

"I'll pay all of what that would be, and I'll pay for the gas," he countered.

"Okay, if you have to. But I go to Raleigh all the time. Or Norfolk. When I'm in power shopping mode, I need a fancier place than Modeste down on Main Street, or any of the dress shops in Elizabeth City. So this conference, it's all about agriculture." She glanced down at the brochure again, then cocked her head at him. "You don't look like the type, Farmer Finn."

He laughed. "I worked for a company that makes pesticides. Except, they have to be toxic for the pests only, not for humans, or for animals that they don't want to poison. So they need chemists to do toxicity testing."

"Sounds complicated."

He nodded.

"How do they do that?"

"If I explained all that—"

"Corporate secrets? You'd have to shoot me?" said Bunny, making her eyes mock-scared. "So, you like that kind of work?"

"It's what I studied for."

"Lotta schooling, to do that."

He nodded.

Bunny looked at him sidelong. "How much schooling?"

"Uh. I have a Ph.D. in biochemistry."

"Sheesh," said Bunny. "I only made it through a year of community college." Farmer Finn. That was a stretch. Dr. Finn, though. It was making her head spin. "Now you want to get back into it, that kind of work," she said instead.

"Not back to what I did for that other company. I ended up—" he paused. "Not liking that work. But there are other things chemists do in agribusiness. I'll go for one of those."

"What didn't you like about the former job, Finn? Aside from the mean boss, that is?"

"For one thing." He stood up and kind of viciously folded the brochure into sections and folded it again. "Animal testing."

"My god, Finn." She thought about his main obsession. "Testing on parrots? You don't mean on parrots."

"Yes, among other animals. Mice, maybe that didn't bother me so much. Uf, that bothered me too. But parrots. They are very intelligent animals, Bunny. So I wouldn't do it. I started becoming a problem for my boss."

"And then. . .she threw you under the bus."

"Yeah." Finn slumped back down. "But I shouldn't have fallen for her. That's on me."

"She got rid of you. Convenient for her, if she thought you were a trouble-maker. Sounds like she had to pick you, or her own career. So she picked—"

"I suppose. Look, can we not talk about this?"

"Sure," said Bunny. Finn was in pain. She had actually learned about that kind of pain. Heartache. In Finn's case, maybe more complicated than mere heartache. Bunny winced. Betrayal, even. Treachery, and from a person he trusted and maybe loved. "But Finn. Why were your objections such a problem? Wouldn't the company be glad you brought it up? Weren't you doing them a favor, pointing it out? Aren't there regulations about stuff like that? Animal cruelty regulations?"

"So many questions." He grimaced. "Regulations for dogs and cats. For a few other animals. The mofos left birds out."

Bunny teared up. "Thinking about Sazarac, somebody hurting him, like poisoning him on purpose—"

"They didn't test on Senegals. But they did use specially-bred budgerigars. Parakeets," he said, at her look of confusion. "But they're still amazing little animals. I wouldn't do it. There was this group, organized to oppose that kind of testing. I joined it."

"And she found out," said Bunny softly. She threw up her hands. "Sorry. Sorry. Sore subject. I won't bring it up again. Let's hit the beach."

Afterward, Finn and Bunny cooked up a delicious dinner together. Finn, it turned out, was much more adventurous than she was when it came to trying new flavors and seasonings.

"Guess it's that bland Minnesota diet. Once I was out of there, you couldn't hold me back."

"Bland? As bland as the usual Southern diet?"

"Blander. Think jello salad. Think walleye. Well, a good walleye right out of the lake, that's good eating. But walleye from the store? Might as well eat Styrofoam. Think of a whole plate with nothing but stuff that's white on it. Think lutefisk."

"Luta what?"

He explained.

"Ewww," said Bunny.

"Exactly," said Finn.

"Although," said Bunny. "Fish soaked in lye. Sounds bad. But hominy is corn soaked in lye, and hominy is de-lish. Grits, mmm-MMM. And grits are just ground-up hominy."

"Ewww," said Finn. He examined the mug in front of him. It read *G.R.I.T.S.* "Grits. You even have a grits mug."

"Stands for Girls Raised In The South," she told him with a smug look. "Still. Fish soaked in lye until it turns into fish jello. I think I'll pass." She had a thought. "Why doesn't food soaked in lye kill you, Dr. Finn?"

"It probably does," said Finn, swatting at her with the pancake turner.

"I will convert you yet, Finn. I know a great shrimp-and-grits place down the coast."

"No wonder you glow in the dark. All that Diet. . .whatever it is, that wine stuff," he told her. "And now I see it. All those lye-soaked grits." He nudged her. "You do, you know." At her look, he went on. "Glow in the dark. I wake up in your bed sometimes, with the moonlight streaming in your bedroom window, and you know what? You glow, Bunny. Like the curve of your cheek, and your shoulder—" He bent over to kiss her shoulder, then ran his scratchy two-day stubble up her cheek.

A whole day of relaxation stretched out before them. They enjoyed it together, as day paled into evening. They played with the animals. Then they headed out to the Currituck Cove community fireworks display. "Bingo, you have to stay behind," said Bunny, petting him. "You know you hate fireworks."

Bingo whined and went into the spare room. By the time they left for the fireworks, Bingo had already crawled far underneath the spare room bed.

After the fireworks, Finn and Bunny took a long walk on the moonlit beach. They went back to Bunny's house for their own fireworks display.

"Okay," said Finn the next morning, after some satisfying additional fireworks. The morning-sex kind. "I'll let you drive me to Raleigh. I'll agree to stay in some fancy hotel with you. But you have to let me pay half."

"You can barely afford the conference fee."

"Yeah, but as soon as I get one of these jobs, I'll be fine. More than fine. Not like I have a mortgage or a family to provide for. Let's do it, Bunny."

"It'll be fun," she promised.

A month later, on the way to Raleigh, Finn was very quiet.

Bunny looked quickly aside at him, then back to highway 64, as it unrolled inland and west toward Raleigh. "Something's wrong."

"Eh."

"Tell me what's wrong. Sheesh, Finn. We're friends, aren't we?" She felt his hand on her thigh, squeezing it.

"Couldn't ask for a better," he said gruffly.

"So tell me."

"She'll probably be at the conference. My former company is based at the Research Triangle. That's why I ended up in North Carolina. She'll be there."

Finn didn't have to say who *she* was. Bunny knew.

"I'll probably run into her my whole career," he said. "I should start getting used to it."

"Not if you just keep working at the UPWD." Bunny giggled, and she got a laugh out of Finn, too.

But actually.

Bunny felt an unexpected twinge.

Actually, she wanted him to keep working at the UPWD, not go off to do some high and mighty Dr. Finn thing.

She was mad at herself for even thinking such a thought. He was a fun fling, he was man-candy for sure.

But it was true, what she'd said. He was her friend. She was his.

And what Finn needed was a place to flex those amazing muscles of his. She tingled at the thought of him and his hot bod. Those muscles, always those. But he needed to flex his brain-power muscles, too, the way she needed—

She said it out loud. "You need a job like this the way I need lipstick."

"Bunny," said Finn. "How can you say something like that."

"I love lipstick."

"Well, I know that. Looks good on you, too. Makes me want to, I dunno, use it like a Magic Marker and draw a Hot Bunny Pink line from here to there—" He reached out a quick finger and drew it from her bellybutton downwards. "—and then lick it off. What say we make edible lipstick next?" His voice was hopeful.

He was silent a beat. His voice turned serious. "But you're making out like you're just some bimbo. And we know that's not true. Both of us know it."

"Wow. Package it in tubes that look like markers. Like in a pack with different colors. Or what about crayons?" She was still thinking about edible lipstick.

He drew his finger down her belly again, right to the top of her crotch, in a light tingling line.

"Stop. You'll make me run off the road." Bunny smiled through the windshield and turned off to the exit for Raleigh.

Just your type

THE NIGHT BEFORE THE conference, Bunny and Finn had a fine time in the king-sized bed of their very nice hotel, using plenty of the little hotel soaps and lotions, and took a relaxing soak in the hot tub after.

The hotel had a shuttle that would drop Finn off at the conference site in the Research Triangle. He had two interviews lined up and got a promise from a grad school mentor of his to have coffee together and strategize about Finn's career.

"This conference fee will more than pay for itself," he told Bunny cheerfully as he headed off on the first morning of the two-day conference.

Bunny boggled after him. She'd only seen Finn in his safari get-up and his biker gear. And the hot red bathing suit. But from somewhere he'd produced a nice suit and dress shirt and tie.

"I have to look professional," he told her.

"You could wear one of those little coats, though."

He grinned at her and closed the hotel room door behind him. She heard his soft footfalls going off down the corridor.

Bunny lay around awhile fantasizing about Finn in a white lab coat and nothing else.

Then she got herself ready and headed out in the hotpinkmobile to one of her favorite boutiques. She'd already had a stern talk with herself about not going full-on shopaholic. She couldn't afford it. Someday, she promised herself, she'd be able to again.

But she was determined to treat herself, at least a little.

When she emerged from the store a few hours later, she was a satisfied customer.

Back at the hotel, she spread out her finds: a great ruffled-sleeve minidress in a bold floral print, very expensive but marked 'way down, and fantastic ankle-strap high-heel sandals in the hot pink she adored.

Jewelry? Didn't need any. She'd brought a little case enclosing Gina's finest designs. Cosmetics? Get out of here! She brought her own lipstick, the Hot Bunny Pink shade, of course, and her carefully-hoarded stash of great Mélisande products, the highest-end her former company sold.

She was due to meet Finn for drinks at the conference center hotel's bar, so she took the shuttle over. No issues with impaired driving that way. Not that she would overdo. "I always have one drink only," she told herself virtuously. "Oh, maybe two."

Once there, she wandered the halls of the monstrous conference center hotel. It was bustling with what she could only assume were earnest science type people. She looked down at her phone.

Meet me outside of Pyramid Room A, Finn had texted. *Session ends at 5pm.*

A little map posted on the hotel directory pointed her to Pyramid Rooms A and B. She trekked for miles, hoping her new shoes wouldn't do a bad number on her feet.

There. There was the hallway. Two anonymous beige doors with signage above. Pyramid Room A. Pyramid Room B. Thank god! Leatherette benches lined the corridor, mostly empty. Bunny sank down on one, grateful to get off her feet. She slipped off the sandals, one at a time, and massaged her insteps. Then she put the sandals back on.

A clock outside the Pyramid Rooms ticked off the time. 4:49.

Good. Bunny hated to be late.

Only a few minutes went by before the doors to both Pyramid Rooms burst open and a stream of people flooded into the corridor.

Finn spotted her. He strode to her and beamed.

She stood, and he leaned in for a kiss. It started out as a mere peck on the lips but somehow became something deeper. He pulled away. "Mind waiting here a little longer? I want to go back in there for a sec—" He tilted his head toward one of the beige doors— "and ask the conference presenter a question."

"Sure. I don't mind. I'll just sit back down on this comfy little bench."

Finn whisked back into Pyramid Room A.

Amid the outpouring from Pyramid Room B, someone turned her head with a hard look for Bunny.

Bunny shifted uncomfortably on her bench. She realized everything about her must scream outsider, her flirty dress, her stylish sandals. These people were all in staid business attire. Besides, PDA in the conference center hallway was probably not cool.

Out of the corner of her eye, Bunny glimpsed the staring woman moving to the wall opposite her and leaning against it as conference-goers streamed past her.

What the flick? thought Bunny. Then told herself she was being silly. This woman—Bunny cast a surreptitious glance at her—was no doubt waiting for someone too. Bunny couldn't shake the bad feeling, though. She imagined everyone in the place doing a double-take, sure she didn't and couldn't belong here.

I'm out of my element, that's all it is, thought Bunny, uncharacteristically nervous. She crossed her legs daintily at the ankles. *I have good ankles*, she told herself, to calm down, *and these sandals show them off well. Good purchase, Bunny Dowdy.*

The woman standing across from her was well-dressed, if kind of starchy looking. A bowed silky blouse under a navy blazer. Gray pencil skirt in a good fabric. Nice legs. The woman's dark hair was pulled back in kind of a severe bun from the lovely oval of her face. *She could use a touch of lipstick. My bold red would be perfect for her.* Bunny imagined sidling up to the woman and handing her a free sample. She almost reached down into her big purse for one. She'd brought several along, and she'd handed them out at the boutique, too. Never waste a marketing opportunity.

Bunny narrowed her eyes. No marketing opportunity with that woman, though. She was lovely. Too bad she looked so unapproachable. *With that skin-tone, she'd wear the bold red so well. She so would.* Bunny hadn't come up with a name for the shade yet. *Executive Red*, maybe? No. Too drab. *Take Control Red?* No. *Dominatrix Red!* Bunny felt her lips curve into a smile. She made herself look away from the woman. It was rude to stare.

Suddenly the woman was right up in Bunny's face. "Kissing Finn Johansen in the middle of the conference, huh? Finn." Her lip curled scornfully. "Some people never change." She turned on her heel and stalked off down the corridor, in a pair of what Bunny could only deplore as very frumpy pumps. *This is a woman who cries out for thigh-high stiletto-heeled leather boots*, Bunny thought. *And a smart little riding crop.*

By the time Finn reappeared, Bunny was shaking. The woman's venom was so sudden. So unexpected.

"What's the matter?" he said.

"Nothing."

"Let's get that drink." He guided her down another long corridor and to a lobby bar.

A couple of people hailed him as he came in, and he waved back at them.

Wow. Here was a new side of Finn.

But Bunny was thinking hard.

By the time they had both settled down at a little table with their sazaracs (in honor of Saz), Bunny was sure she understood what she had just experienced, back there in the hallway outside the Pyramid Rooms. That woman. That woman and her scorn and her rudeness. That had been HER. That had been Finn's evil bus-flattening, neck-slashing, backstabbing former boss.

She opened her mouth to say something. Then she closed it again. Finn was over the moon. He'd just had a great conversation with one of the leading lights in his field. *Don't say anything to knock that confidence out of him*, she thought.

"He really got my question," Finn told Bunny, echoing her thoughts. "Restores the confidence, you know?"

Bunny smiled at him and took a careful sip of her drink. "The expert?"

"Right. And I had lunch with my grad school mentor. She's so smart. She was full of good ideas about how I can re-start my career."

"What about the interviews?"

"Tomorrow," Finn said. "Glad I had the conversation with my mentor first. Now I'll go into those interviews with a lot more confidence."

"Where are those jobs?"

"One is in Portland."

"Oregon?" said Bunny.

"Yeah, and the other is in San Diego."

"Oh. Cool," said Bunny. Inside, a little voice was going, *It's Paris all over again.* She shook the thought off. This wasn't Paris, what she and Finn had. Finn was a party in safari shorts. Everywoman's fantasy of the hot delivery guy showing up on her porch with his big package.

So what if he was actually some serious scientist.

She could pretend not to think about that.

Besides, the little voice told her, *soon he'll be gone.*

"Bunny." Finn leaned forward and put his hand over hers. "I've come to know you pretty well. Something's wrong."

"No, it's not," she said. "I hope Ada is doing okay with Bingo and Saz. Saz can be a handful."

"That's what's worrying you?"

"Oh, I'm sure it will be fine," said Bunny brightly.

Finn stared across the table at her, a crease of concern between his eyes. "Ada's a good kid." He studied her. "That's not what's worrying you."

But then a few people came to their table, and Finn stood up. "Hi, guys!" he said. "This is Bunny Dowdy, a good friend of mine." He told her all their names and rapidly explained what they all did. Sounded like gobbledygook to Bunny. Stuff involving laboratories and chemistry, no doubt. "We're just about to get something to eat," Finn said to them. "Join us?"

They spent a good three hours at dinner, Finn and his friends laughing and talking over old times, while Bunny sat quietly in the corner of the restaurant booth.

The food was kind of mediocre. Even the décor was lackluster. But it was clear Finn and his friends didn't care. They were too busy catching up to think about food. They lingered over the dinner, lingered over kind of bad coffee served in generic looking cups right out of the restaurant supply place. Even shared a few desserts.

Finally they were ready to leave. Bunny was more than ready. One of the friends insisted on paying. "Look, man, I just got the big promotion."

Finn was gracious with his thanks, but to Bunny, his smile looked a bit bitter.

On the shuttle back to their own hotel, he was quiet.

Once they were in their room, Bunny put her hands on his shoulders. He had slumped down on the side of the bed. "Right back at you, Finn. Something's wrong. I can tell."

"I shouldn't have let George pay," he said.

"Come on. George wanted to pay."

"Yeah, but those three knew what happened to me. They feel sorry for me. I don't like that."

"Finn. Friends look out for each other. Suppose it was George who'd gotten thrown under the bus? Wouldn't you have helped him?"

"Yeah."

"So."

"So, you're right, Bunny." He smiled up at her, but his smile was wan.

"Pretty soon, you'll have a good job again, and you can pay it forward."

"Everyone knows what happened to me, though," he said. "Some people aren't gonna understand. They're gonna think I maybe did something wrong. I may not get those jobs, even though—" He slammed one hand into the other. "—they're exactly right for me, especially the Portland one."

"You don't know they'll think you did anything wrong," said Bunny. "All you can do is go in there and blow them away in the interview. Then, if it goes wrong, and that's why it goes wrong, it's on them."

"I'll think about that while I'm delivering packages in my stupid safari getup," said Finn.

She dimpled. "I love you in the stupid safari getup."

"You would," said Finn, beginning to smile too. He pulled her down beside him onto the bed's lush comforter.

But she turned aside when he tried to kiss her. She teared up.

"Oh, now. Something's wrong, Bunny Dowdy. You have to tell me."

She couldn't tell him about the woman in the hallway. She just couldn't. "Your friends probably all think I'm some airhead," she said instead.

"They don't think that."

"How do you know they don't?"

"Because I know them, and they don't pigeonhole people that way. Besides, they're jealous as hell."

Bunny giggled. "Even Leona?"

"Especially Leona. She's gay. She was probably the most jealous of the bunch. You're exactly her type."

By then, Bunny had loosened Finn's tie and kicked off her sandals. The two of them shed the rest of their nice clothes, and then they whooped it up in the big king-sized bed.

In the afterglow, they lay in each other's arms. "So I'm just Leona's type, am I?" Bunny teased. Then she sobered. "But I'm not yours. Am I."

"Bunny—" Finn rose on an elbow, searching her with his eyes. "Why would you say that?"

"Just a feeling. I bet you don't go for blondes."

"Not usually," said Finn. "I guess not usually. But I go for you." He kissed her, but he'd turned serious, too. "I have a bad feeling about tomorrow's interviews. I have to wonder—"

"Wonder what?"

"Whether she's sabotaging me."

Bunny stared at him.

"My former boss," he elaborated. "Rona Petreius. That's her name."

So Bunny knew she was right. He was thinking about that woman, just as she thought he might be. *Rona Petreius.* Bunny attached the name to the woman. *That's the type of woman Finn usually goes for.* She knew it instinctively. Dark-haired, flawless ivory skin. Tall. Severe. Scary smart. "You think she's bad-mouthing you," she said.

"I think she might be. Something George let slip."

I think she might be, too, Finn, thought Bunny. She didn't say anything. Just pulled him close.

Whatta package

"PACKAGING'S HALF THE battle," Bunny instructed Finn. "The product has to be superb. Of course it does. Great package, shoddy product? That breaks the contract the packaging has made with your customer."

"It does?" said Finn, fiddling with a miniature stainless steel implement, getting an exact fix on some tiny amount of a powder and sliding it into a mixture he was experimenting with. "I think I'm going to be able to get you an amazing mauve," he told her.

"Yeah, see," said Bunny, talking past him. "The package is a promise. If the package says, *Quality product here!* and then doesn't live up to the promise, no repeat customers."

"So, really, packaging isn't that important."

"Yes, it is. They both have to work in tandem. Packaging. And product. Without an enticing package, no cosmetics customer will bother. Without an enticing product, she won't come back for seconds. Both/and."

"I see."

"And then." Bunny blew out a sigh. "Well. Pricing, that's an art in itself. If you price a cosmetic too low, your customer will think, cheap price, cheap product. And the customer, see, wants to look like a million bucks. So, it's kinda counter-intuitive, but you need to set your price high enough. I mean, Adorable Me—moderate price. Adorée—more expensive. Mélisande? So expensive it scorches your eyebrows off. And it's all more or less the same stuff."

"That sounds like a scam," said Finn, scowling.

"It does, doesn't it? You know, I think most customers actually know that, what I just said about it all being the same stuff. But if they can afford it, they go for the expensive stuff every time."

"That IS counter-intuitive."

"It's like they're not buying a product so much as they're buying a self-image. So this—" Bunny tapped the little sample Finn held out for her to see. "—this isn't just some mauve goo. This is *I Want To Feel Good*. This is *I Want Self-Confidence*."

"Hi, y'all. Sorry to butt in. You left your door open a crack."

Bunny and Finn leaped to their feet.

"Just wanted to come over and be neighborly and all."

"Well, hey, you," said Bunny. "This is Finn, Brenda. He helps me out in here sometimes."

The tiny woman who had just popped in, all huge eyes and hair down to there, grinned at Finn. "Oh, I know," she said. She winked.

Damn, thought Bunny. But she controlled her voice and expression. "And Finn, this is Brenda Hutchinson. We went to high school together."

"Hi." Brenda stuck out a hand, and Finn shook it. "I'm Florella Spiritsong. I go by that now," she said to Bunny. "Brought you a little housewarming present." She thrust something at Bunny. A grass-green mug.

"Thanks Brenda! Uh. Florella," said Bunny, scrutinizing the mug. *Florella Spiritsong, Self-Actualization*, in a flowing script, was inscribed on the back, plus a businesslike web address. On the front, *Be Kind! Be Grateful! Be Happy! Be YOU!*

"I couldn't help overhearing what you just said, Bunny," Brenda/Florella said. "How it's not all lipstick. It's self-awareness, am I right? That's what I do, too." She turned to Finn. "I don't just sell soap. I sell self-actualization."

Finn picked up the mug and read its message. He raised an eyebrow. "So I see."

"And hey, Finn," she went on, not noticing his tone, "I see you heading over to the Truckers' DLite with your towel. Figure you might need one of my soaps." She handed him a little flat waxy block. "Word to the wise. Don't use the stuff in the dispensers."

"I don't," he said, his lips twitching, "but thanks for the soap. I can always use soap."

"Yeah, it's a great product, soap. My soap, it's a party in a little scented package, but it's a necessity, too, know what I mean? It's a staple. It's a consumer product. Like toothpaste. Or toilet paper. Recession-proof. But cute. If you have to buy a staple, why not buy a cute staple?"

"Exactly," said Bunny. "I love my scented soaps." Then, casting a quick look at Finn, "Although I don't use them any more. An allergy thing," she said as Florella/Brenda frowned.

"Well, you know—" Florella produced another little sample and pressed it on Bunny. "—I do have my hypoallergenic scent-free line."

"Wow," said Bunny. "I'd like to hear about that. I want to make a cosmetics line like that."

"Let's do lunch," said Florella/Brenda. "Bye!" She disappeared out the door with a flutter of her hand.

Bunny rushed to door and latched it. "They're on to us, Finn."

"And," said Finn, "I'd say nobody cares."

"So," Bunny went on briskly. "We were talking about packaging." Finn was in his biker shorts. She took a quick look. Took a breath. Whatta package. "So then there's distribution. That's a biggie, too. If you don't have a way, a place, to sell your product, it can be the best product in the world but if you can't get it to the people who you know would love to have it, you are so fucked."

"Don't you have to advertise, all that?"

"All the promotion part. Whew. Makes me want to take a nap, just thinking about it. And Finn—this marketing stuff was done FOR me when I was an Adorable Me rep. I didn't have to think about any of it. Or not much. Sometimes I feel overwhelmed, you know?"

"You can do it, Bunny Dowdy." He sniffed the soap sample. "Gaaaah."

"Here, have mine," said Bunny. "We'll trade."

"I don't want that thing anywhere near Saz," he said ominously.

"Watch this, Finn." Bunny waltzed to the trash can. She dropped the scented sample in. "See that? See there? Good parrot parent."

"Well, all righty, then," he said.

"It'll make our trash smell nice."

"So I don't get it, what you just said. I mean, you told me Adorable Me went under because the company raised its prices and went for the high end."

"I'm talking in general, Finn. I mean, the whole marketing segmentation thing is pretty complicated. Adorable Me worked because it homed in ruthlessly on one type of customer, the type who wants a nice little package, but value, value, value. When Adorable Me went upscale, you can bet I told all my old customers just to keep buying Adorable Me, because they were getting the same stuff at a nice affordable price. But to my new fancy customers—well, that was a different story."

"Still sounds like a scam."

"I guess it would be, if all these people weren't capable of thinking it through for themselves. And they were. And they did. They do. They buy what they decide they need—cosmetics, yes. Image, yes. 'Thrifty homemaker—but I deserve to look good'? Yes, you deserve it, and let me help you look good. Here's an economical version of a great product. 'What a fancy, trendy person I am—and I don't care how much it costs'? Yes, you are, and let me help you flaunt it. Here's the top of the line with the fancy package that will look so good on your vanity. And when you take it out of your purse at the country club, in front of the other ladies who lunch? Whooooo-eee, girl. You've arrived."

"So you do know what you're doing. You know your customer. You actually like your customer."

"Yep. Unfortunately, a lot of the Adorable Me reps didn't realize they'd have to sell the different lines differently. And the company didn't give them enough help seeing what they had to do. So we all went down with the ship together." Bunny looked at him sidelong. "I feel frivolous saying this stuff to you, Finn. I mean, you stood up for parrots!"

Finn rolled his eyes. "And look how much good it did me."

"We wouldn't have met, if you hadn't."

He nodded slowly, fixing her with his eye. "Yeah. You're right, Bunny. And that would have been a tragedy."

"A tragedy?"

"Bunny—you and I, we—"

"Oh, now, Finn," she turned away, a little scared. She couldn't start feeling that way about Finn. The Paris way. "Let's just—"

"Yeah," he said. After a moment, "I heard from those two labs. They said no, both of them."

"Aww, Finn. Do you think that woman did you in with them?"

"Not sure about one of them. I know so, about the one in Port-land. George told me."

"That was the one you really wanted."

He nodded. "Oh, well. The job I told you about a while back? The one in Minnesota? The company's run by my mother's cousin. That one's still a possibility. I hate to think I'd get a job that way. Sounds kind of desperate. But I am, Bunny." His eyes burned into hers. "I am desperate. Who am I kidding? If it comes through, I'm going to take it."

"When will you hear?" No point telling him half the world got jobs through their personal connections. No point reminding him job-seeker advice always starts with, *Use every contact you have.* In his world, people got jobs through their superior chemistry chops, or something crazy like that, nothing any normal person would think of. Except—someone's malice could derail the whole thingamabob, apparently. No point telling him this dark side of his kind's own job-seeking methods, either. He already knew about it, and in the worst, most personal way.

Also no point telling him her heart had just dropped into her shoes, and one of her stiletto heels was stabbing right through it. Minnesota was really far away. Somehow, Portland and San Diego had seemed unreal. Minnesota, though. It sounded real. It sounded like it was going to happen, and then Finn would go away.

"I'll hear maybe as soon as next week. So." He turned back to the table, and the supplies. "So, just in case I'm not here to see you through, I want to leave you in great shape, Bunny. I'll get you all squared away with your formulas, and then I'll pay off the rest of the six-months' rent and you'll have a little nest egg to draw on for all that expensive packaging."

You're the package I want, Finn, thought Bunny. It scared her to think it, because she wasn't thinking about THAT package at all. Or, well, of course that. But mostly she was thinking about the total Finn package. All of him. What he was coming to mean to her.

You're swimming in dangerous waters, Bunny Dowdy, she told herself, *and a riptide's coming up on you fast.*

Fly away

"I'LL DRIVE YOU TO THE airport. Norfolk or Raleigh?" Bunny said.

"I can get a cheaper flight from RDU but it will be quicker for you to take me to Norfolk," said Finn. "It's not that big a difference. I'll book from Norfolk. You sure you want to—"

"Of course I want to." *No no no no no.* "What are friends for?"

"I'll fly to Minnesota, use it as an excuse to see my folks, interview with Farmington Toxicology, and then—then I'm not sure."

"You're not coming back to get your stuff?"

"Nah, I'll box it all up and take it to the UPWD. Sarabeth will hold it for me behind the counter. Then, if she needs to, she can send it on. And if I bomb the interview, I'll make a quick trip back and grab it myself."

Sarabeth, the gum-cracking teen counter-clerk. She wasn't so bad. Nice kid, actually.

"So what about your boss? Will he let you just go off to interview?"

"I thought of telling him some lie about a family crisis and could I please have leave. But I put in my notice instead."

"You're pretty sure you'll get this job."

"You know, Bunny, I'm not sure. So I may come back here, my tail between my legs, and try to get you to let me move back onto my cot."

"You pay your rent. You've held up your side of our bargain. Of course you can come back."

93

"But then I'll have to look for another shit job around here. So—" His shoulders sagged. "It will make more sense if I stay up there and look for a shit job in The Cities."

By now, Bunny knew that The Cities were the Twin Cities, Minneapolis and Saint Paul.

"I could live with my folks." He turned to her. "Nothing I'd ever want to do. I left home for college and never looked back. But I might have to swallow my pride and move back in with the folks. I'll still pay the rest of the rent I owe you, Bunny, no matter what."

"Oh, well, only two months of it left. Then I'll have to make a decision. Go all in, renew my lease, put everything on the line, or look for my own shit job." Bunny tried to laugh.

Finn wasn't fooled. He hugged her tight. "I'm gonna miss you, Bunny."

"I'll miss you, too. But far be it from me to stand in the way of science."

"It's just what I do, Bunny."

"Well, I know that," she said. "It's what you are, Finn. That's important."

"You know," he said slowly. "You could come—"

Bunny put a hand over his mouth. "Don't even say it, Finn. That wouldn't work out. You know that." *Even when my heart was breaking in Paris, I knew that,* she thought. *I could have stayed over there with Etienne. But I didn't. I couldn't.* "I belong here at the beach."

"Yeah. You do. I can't imagine you not living at the beach."

Bunny and Finn were talking Finn's momentous decision out over coffee at Bunny's little kitchen table. Bunny looked down dully at her plain white mug that read in generic black lettering *I went to Paris and all I got was this lousy mug.*

It was a quiet Sunday morning. Bingo dozed at their feet, managing to overlap both sets of toes with his comforting doggie body. Bingo knew. *Dogs do know*, thought Bunny. Bingo knew something important was up, and he knew both his humans needed comfort.

That in itself was interesting—and painful. Bingo thought of them both as his humans now. Bunny more than Finn, but after his first suspicions of Finn, Bingo had gone all in. Finn was an animal lover, and Bingo knew that right down to his doggie bones. Every animal Finn came across knew that. No wonder he couldn't stand having to work in animal testing.

Bingo's gonna be sad, Bunny thought.

One person who was not sad in that household? Sazarac. He was turning out to be the world's happiest parrot. When he was allowed out, he enjoyed himself. Then he was more than content to go back to his cage, because he knew Bunny or Finn would make sure treats were in there waiting for him.

"Good birrrrrrd," he'd say.

He had also decided he liked perching on Bunny's shoulder and giving her tiny love bites on the neck, and preening her. Or, better yet, unraveling her sweater or teeshirt at the neck.

"Sazzie. No." Bunny would scold.

It didn't stop Sazarac from trying.

"Sazzie is really smart," Bunny told Finn now. "Bingo is sad. He knows something is up between us. So why doesn't Sazzie?"

"He probably doesn't know us well enough yet. But when I leave—"

"Yeah," said Bunny softly. "Then he'll be sad."

"Bunny, look. We knew this day was gonna come."

"That doesn't make it any easier," Bunny told him, not meeting his eye. "You know, I started out giving myself a little talking to, like how you and I, well, it's just for fun, you know? But now." She couldn't go on without tearing up, and she didn't want to tear up. If she teared up, she would bawl her eyes out, and that was unfair to Finn. She wanted only the best for Finn. She laughed a little. "You probably don't feel the same way."

"Bunny." He hitched his chair over so he could take her in his arms. "I do feel the same way, Bunny. But I have to go."

"I know. Your career. And to you, it's not just a career. It's a calling. I've come to see that."

"You have a calling, too, Bunny."

She managed a smile. "I do not."

"Yeah, you do. I've been thinking about that a lot. Thinking about how much I'd love it if you came with me. But then thinking, nope, that wouldn't work. Because you do have a calling."

She shook her head.

"You do. It has taken me the longest time to figure out what it is. It's about being Bunny. Being one of a kind. You are, you know. You're the most one-of-a-kind person I've ever known."

"Oh, now."

"It's true. And the beach is part of you. I know you told me about that guy in Paris. So. Why not stay in Paris? Especially because, by then, you were getting those vibes you told me about."

"The vibes that Adorable Me was on a downhill slide. You're right. By then I was starting to realize."

"So why not stay with that man you had fallen for? What was keeping you?"

"I just couldn't."

"Yeah, and I know why. It's the beach, Bunny. Some people, they have roots. Not the kind you get from inertia and laziness, like, I've lived here all my life and I have so little imagination I can't think of ever living anywhere else. That's my parents," he muttered. "Uf. Maybe unfair to think that about them. But Bunny, your roots are real. You're one of those people who has a feel for a place so hard and deep that it's part of you. That's what you have, Bunny."

"That makes me sound like something I'm not, Finn. I'm just the kind of person who wants to party through life."

"And that's a lie, Bunny Dowdy. Wow. I know you better than you know yourself. Sure, you love to party and have fun, and I sure love to have fun with you. But that's not all you are. That's just the tip of the Bunny Iceberg."

He hugged her tight.

Oh, well, with Finn, one hug leads to another, and another, and then, pretty soon. . .so a few hours later they woke up from wonderful naps, lazy and relaxed in Bunny's bed.

Bunny turned to him and ran a finger down his cheek. "I sure am gonna miss this, Finn. But next week, I'll drive you to the airport, and I'll be cheerleading at long distance through your interview, and hoping it all goes well, and hoping you get that job."

"I'm thinking it will be a pretty drab job," he confessed.

"But you'll do great work for them. And you'll keep those antennae out and use that job as a platform to go on to more interesting work."

"Yeah. I don't want to take their job if I can't put my best into it, though."

"But you will, Finn. Lordy, look what you've been doing for me, and you don't even like the cosmetics industry. Much less some little cosmetics startup behind the UPWD in some podunk town."

Finn winced. "I did call Currituck Cove that, didn't I? I was wrong. This is a beautiful, close-knit little community. I've made friends here."

Bunny giggled. "You are a serious scientist—" She made a very stick-up-the-ass face at him—"and here you are, helping out a frivolous woman in the most frivolous of all industries."

Finn rolled over and pinned her to the bed. "You are not" He poked her. "a frivolous woman."

I'm just not your woman, Bunny thought sadly. *That horrible boss is more your type. And she did you dirty.* Bunny called up a picture of the woman. Rona Petreius, Finn had said her name was. The beauty of her skin. Her very severe brand of beauty, just begging for a slash of scarlet across that mouth of hers. *Maybe I'll call that shade Rona Red.* She had to giggle. Then the name burst on Bunny in a Patented Bunny Bolt From the Blue. *Like a Boss Red!*

"What goes on in that alien mind of yours?" Finn wondered aloud. He leaned down and kissed her. He made quite the project out of the kiss, exploring her tongue and lips with his. Then moving to plant little kisses down her neck. "Mmmmm," he said, as his mouth found her breasts.

Her nipples had risen to the challenge, tingling in anticipation.

He made a line of kisses down the middle of her, to her navel, rolling his tongue around it. Then kisses, serious kisses, around another part of her tingling and wet and wanting him. And his tongue exploring inside.

She helped him roll the condom on, admiring his erection, the purply veins, the velvet pink head, pulsing with desire. And guided him inside her, wriggling him closer until he filled her completely.

Their love noises filled the house.

"How am I gonna live without this?" he groaned, rolling off her.

"You'll manage." She patted his shoulder, the solid muscle of it, making her tingle all over again. *Not sure I will*. She made the words stay inside her head.

A week later, she was driving him to Norfolk. They didn't say much to each other on the trip over. What could they say, really?

In the departure lane, he grabbed his backpack from the back seat, and slid out the mammoth carton that contained his bike.

His Surly bike, she thought with a reminiscent smile.

He poked his head back in for a last kiss. "Wish I could afford one of those hard-shelled bike cases," he fretted. "But working at the UPackWeDeliver panned out for me in that way, at least. They have good cardboard bike boxes, and I got the insurance discounted."

"It'll be fine, Finn," she said.

"Take care of Sazzie," he said.

"You know I will."

"Text me or email me the second you have a problem."

"I will."

"Wish I could have spent more time with Bingo."

"You're stalling, Safari Man. Go fly away."

"I know. I hate this part. Saying goodbye." He gave her a quick kiss. Then he was gone.

An impatient driver behind Bunny leaned on his horn, so she swung out of the drop-off lane. But a little bit down the highway, she had to pull over and have a good cry.

Stormy weather

AT THE END OF HER LEASING period, Bunny re-upped with leasing agent Chet Martin for a year.

This could be a big mistake, thought Bunny, signing Chet's contract. She had yet to make a dime in sales. But the six-month lease was only available as a teaser, so sign up for a year or give up the Lipstick Factory. She was running through her savings in a hurry.

Somehow, a little voice told her she needed to put in more time before calling it quits. She paid attention to that voice. It had never steered her wrong yet, not where cosmetics were involved.

At least now she had a solid product. Three lipstick shades, in a lovely consistency. Great staying power, too. She rotated them around, wearing one of them herself every day. And the ingredients were all organic, and vegan, too. She planned to use that as a selling point. Right now, all three had nice environmentally friendly fragrances, but as soon as she got around to it, she would have that lunch with Florella/Brenda and email Finn for some tips. Then she'd create a fragrance-free line.

Right now, she was wearing her very favorite. Hot Bunny Pink. Of course it was. She pressed a little sample tub of it on Chet for his wife.

Then she stepped out of his office into the mild October air and headed for home to walk Bingo and feed Sazzie.

The weather was holding. October at the beach could be a lovely time. The only threatening hurricane had turned inland at the last minute and slowed down, so all they had in Currituck Cove was a big rain. A different hurricane had walloped Florida's Gulf Coast in mid-September. The Carolina beaches escaped.

For a whole week, everything had been calm and sunny. The big rollers of waves had hissed and foamed up onto the beach, sighed back out to sea, rolled in again in the age-old, soothing rhythm she loved.

Bunny had traveled quite a bit in her time as the top-ranked Adorable Me sales rep. She knew what it was like to go to sleep and wake up without that ocean sound, or the tang of ocean breezes. The best feeling in the whole world was coming back home to them again.

Her friend Gina missed the beach, but she was happy in the mountains. Their other friend, Fran, hadn't moved inland very far, but in Elizabeth City, she didn't live within earshot of the ocean the way Bunny did.

"Finn was right about me," Bunny told Bingo. "The beach. This is where my heart is."

Bingo whined.

Bunny was about to put his leash on him. "I know, I know. Where's Finn?" she said, tousling his ears.

From the living room scratched a voice. "Wherrrrre's Finn. Wherrrrre's Finn."

"Oh, Saz," Bunny called. "You miss him too."

Everything wasn't gloom and doom, though. The very next day, Bunny got a call from Franklin Nesbit. Franklin was the richest man in Currituck Cove, with a big house in the stately neighborhood bordering the nature preserve, and another mammoth house on the beach, down at the far fancy end.

"Ms. Dowdy? Franklin Nesbit here."

"Why, hey, Mr. Nesbit. How ya doing?"

"Doing good. Listen, Bunny. Ms. Dowdy."

"Bunny is fine," said Bunny with a giggle. "Makes me feel old when you call me Ms. Dowdy." Bunny had gone to high school with Mr. Nesbit's ne'er-do-well son, Bo. A hard partier. At one time, Bunny had done some hard partying with Bo herself, although they'd never had a thing for each other.

"So, Bunny, I was sorry to hear about your franchise going under. Bad break."

"Yes, sir. It sure was."

"But I hear you have a little enterprise of your own in mind."

Bunny didn't ask where he had heard. Currituck Cove was a small town, and everyone was up in everybody else's business, personal and otherwise.

"Yessir, I sure do," said Bunny. "I'm making my own cosmetics. I'm just getting the company off the ground."

"Well, now, Bunny, I'd like to talk to you about that."

Bunny was floored. "Why, sure, Mr. Nesbit. I'll be tickled to talk to you about The Lipstick Goddess." There. She'd just officially named it.

Three days later, dressed in her best, she was sashaying past the other lunchers to join Mr. Nesbit at his table in the Currituck Cove Country Club's faded dining room.

Mr. Nesbit stood. "Glad you could join me, Bunny." He held out her chair. "Would've invited you over to the new golf club, but their dining room is closed for renovations."

They ate an excellent lunch together. As they finished, Mr. Nesbit got down to business. He'd heard about her great idea. He was looking to invest in a local business, and was wondering if she'd go for a silent partnership arrangement.

As he talked over what he had in mind, Bunny was dazzled. Yes, of course she'd go for that! *Wow*, she thought. *A source of capital. I'm all set!*

"Good, good. Let's meet with my lawyer in a week and hash out the details."

As he called for the check, he turned to Bunny. "By the way, Bo sends his regards."

"How's Bo doing? We had some good times in high school." She could have bit her tongue.

"Too good," he said, looking a little grim.

She summoned up a smile. "And now we're grown-ups. All that's behind us."

As the week went by and Bunny met with Mr. Nesbit's lawyer, she began to get a sinking feeling.

It was about Bo Nesbit, Mr. Nesbit's son.

Bo had failed at just about everything his father expected him to do. College. Several of those. Two or three different kinds of businesses. Real estate. Insurance. Finally Mr. Nesbit had given in to his son's only interest, fishing. He funded Bo's ambition to run fishing expeditions out of Corolla, catering to wealthy tourists.

That was something Bo was actually good at, or so everyone said. Something he actually wanted to do. So Bunny, along with all the rest of the people who had gone to high school with Bo, figured Bo had finally found his niche.

In one way, though, Bo had not changed.

Gaaah, Bunny thought. *I even set Gina up with Bo, that one time. She near about murdered me.*

Bo was all hands.

Now, ordinarily, that was fine with Bunny. But the all-hands thing had to be based on mutual attraction, not just Bo getting drunk as a skunk and unilaterally deciding you needed his hands all over you, his stale beer breath in your face, and his tongue trying to force itself down your throat.

The only time Bunny had ever dated Bo, Bunny had spent the whole date fending him off. Actually slapping him at the end of it.

In high school!

Then, when Gina reported back to Bunny and Fran almost three decades later, Bo had outraged Gina with the very same handsy shit.

Bo had two failed marriages behind him. Both wives had huffed off when they caught him with other women. The first wife, when she'd caught him with the woman who became his second. The second, when she'd caught a disease and realized it came by way of Bo from the town's second-biggest loser, Miranda Smythe.

The town's first-biggest loser was, of course, Bo.

Bo was a good-looking guy. His only other success, besides running the sports fishing boat, had been as the fullback on the Currituck Cove High varsity team. Go, Crabbers! But now that big fullback body was starting to run to fat.

All the beer. All the pork rinds. All the Krispy Kremes. All the trips to Biscuitville.

He carried the weight well, being tall and broad and all. He still made the ladies' heads turn as they passed him on the street. If they were from out of town and didn't know him, that is. Or, Bunny guessed, if they were Miranda Smythe.

And Bo was a rich kid. An only child. All Mr. Nesbit's wealth would one day be Bo's.

As Bunny puttered about the Lipstick Lab one morning, her phone burred and she answered it before she thought to look at the caller ID.

Damn. Bo.

"Hey, Miss Bunny. My dad says you asked about me," he said.

"Well, hey back, Bo."

"I hear you and my dad got some business thing going on."

"Looks like it," said Bunny, feeling cautious.

"Look, Dad is throwing a little picnic, before the weather turns. You know. The one he throws every year down at the beach house. He thought maybe I could escort you to it."

Bunny's mind whirred. She needed to stay good with Mr. Nesbit, and Mr. Nesbit's annual beach party was the highlight of the Currituck Cove business community's socializing. All the movers and shakers would be there. Where was the harm in letting Bo take her to this party? *Picnic, not exactly,* she snorted. So she said yes.

She wore her flirty floral dress, the one she had gotten in Raleigh. *When I was there with Finn,* she thought with a pang. But she put on more sensible shoes, low cork-soled sandals, because the party would be down on the beach, a late afternoon-into-early-evening thing with a bonfire. All the Chamber of Commerce people would be there. And business folks from up and down the beach communities from Albemarle Sound on the Virginia line all the way down to the northernmost of the South Carolina beaches.

Bo would be a necessary evil. Bunny could make a lot of contacts at a party like that. She needed those. So. Let Bo take her to it.

When Bo swung by to pick her up in his Range Rover, a bold yellow, Bunny sighed with pleasure, even though she had to giggle at what Suzanne had said, down at the bakery. *Like a big ole stick a buttah on wheels.*

By the time Bunny and Bo got down the coast to the Nesbit family's beachfront property, Bunny was no longer giggling. She was suppressing whimpers of fear instead. Sweaty palms, the whole bit.

Bo had clearly had quite a few before he picked Bunny up. Quite the head start on the party.

They arrived at the Nesbit beach house intact, in spite of wavering all over the highway and crossing the center line at least twice. Bunny stumbled from the car and soon had her own drink in hand.

I need this to steady my nerves, she thought. She gulped it down. A tall mojito.

Pitchers of them paraded down long tables set up at the edge of the beach, with white-coated minions to pour them, and a full bar at the end for anyone who craved anything different.

"Miss Bunny Dowdy," said Mr. Nesbit, coming to greet her. "As pretty as a picture." He led her up the path from the beach to Mrs. Nesbit, her regal self, lounging in an Adirondack chair on the veranda of the big Nesbit beach house, a carafe of martinis at her elbow.

So that's where Bo gets it, thought Bunny. She'd grown up with these people, but she'd never understood what she now saw in Mrs. Nesbit's glassy eyes.

"Why, hello, Miss Bunny," slurred Mrs. Nesbit. "I don't think I've seen you since you were a little girl running round the beach with Bo."

Not true, thought Bunny. *Just last year, I sold you a shit-ton of Mélisande.* But she knew that to Mrs. Nesbit, she was more or less the help, and it was beneath Mrs. Nesbit to remember every one of the little people who served her needs.

Don't care, Bunny told herself. Bunny had cashed Mrs. Nesbit's big check, and she was glad to do it, too. She smiled carefully back at Mrs. Nesbit, wishing she could whisk the woman inside and redo her lipstick, which had collected in the creases radiating from her lips, giving her a distinctly mummified appearance.

"I'm so grateful you're with Bo," Mr. Nesbit murmured at Bunny's ear, leading her back to the beach. "What that boy need's a steadying influence. I want you to be friends with my son, Bunny. I know y'all were friends in high school. Why, I'd just love it if you two renewed your friendship." He patted her hand and turned aside to greet some of his high-flying guests.

So that's it, thought Bunny. *Silent partnership, my ass.* Mr. Nesbit had some scheme in mind. Throw Bunny and Bo together, anything to get his scoundrelly son settled down. And Bunny wasn't even one of the country club set that Mr. Nesbit surely wished Bo would marry. No one in that set would have Bo. Mr. Nesbit was willing to settle for Bunny as his third in a series of daughters-in-law. Mr. Nesbit was that desperate.

And he thinks I can be bought, thought Bunny, beginning to move from outraged to outright furious.

Right then, she started scheming about how she could leave the party as soon as possible without making a scene. *I mean*, she told herself, *maybe I'm wrong.* She sure did need Mr. Nesbit's infusion of cash. So if she were wrong, she wouldn't want to offend him.

But something inside her told her she was right.

Ugh. There was Bo. He'd spotted her, and now he was lurching toward her, drink in hand. She'd bet money it wasn't his first since they'd arrived at the big spread on the beach. When he reached Bunny, he gripped her about the upper arm with his big meaty hand.

"Ow, Bo. Let go. That hurts," said Bunny.

Bo leered into her face and tried to plant a kiss on her as Bunny twisted away.

"You heard the lady. Let go of her." A cool voice behind Bo.

"You're the big man now," Bo sneered.

Bunny turned around to see who was coming to her rescue. "Charlie!" she screeched.

"Hey, Bunny. Haven't seen you since high school."

The last time Bunny had seen Charlie Pounder, he'd been a nerdy guy in glasses, the smartest one in their class. Their high school valedictorian. Everyone liked him, but he never came to their parties, just the last party of their high school years, right after graduation, and he hadn't stayed long, and he'd brought a date nobody knew.

Then he'd gone off to Raleigh for college. Later, law school. Now he was some big-time Raleigh lawyer, and Bunny could see it written all over him. Prosperity. Nothing vulgar, that wasn't Charlie. But clearly, he had made it big.

Bo let go of Bunny. Now he lurched for the mojitos. Charlie steered Bunny away from him.

"Lordy, Bunny. Bo? You're too smart for Bo."

Bunny made a face. "I'm maybe going into business with Mr. Nesbit, and somehow, he boxed me into letting Bo take me to his beach party."

"He's already soaked, and getting wetter," said Charlie. "Don't let him drive you home."

"I'm not gonna. I'm amazed we got to the party alive." Bunny shuddered and grinned at Charlie. But when she thought of her mother, she realized it was no laughing matter, and Charlie—she narrowed her eyes. Charlie saw it, too. "What have you been up to, Charlie?" Charlie didn't need to hear all Bunny's problems. She tactfully changed the subject from Bo. Bunny had always liked Charlie. He was divorced now, she heard.

"This and that. Nothing special."

Moving into his forties had improved Charlie, Bunny decided. The weedy, dorky look was gone. He had become a good-looking man. *Hey, we've all improved*, thought Bunny. *Most of us*. She cast a quick look around for Bo. Big relief, didn't see him anyplace close by.

She and Charlie chatted for a while."Come over to Raleigh much?" he said.

"A little. I like to shop there, but Norfolk's closer."

"Next time you head in my direction, let me know. I'll show you around."

Bunny said she would. She was beginning to enjoy herself. It might be fun to reconnect with Charlie, the new Charlie. He wasn't fling material, though.

Then she felt guilty. Why was she thinking about flings with other men? She was missing Finn.

Charlie leaned over to mock-whisper. "Don't look now, but here comes Bo."

Bunny giggled. "I am going to circulate. Circulate myself right away from Bo. Great seeing you again, Charlie."

"Call me," he said, thrusting a card at her as she edged away into the thick of the beach partiers and away from the oncoming Bo, a massive wall of meat bearing down on her.

Bunny had decided. It was nice seeing Charlie, it might be nice to talk to him a little longer, but not with Bo behaving the way he was. Bo was being a big pita. Too drunk to do anything but paw her, not drunk enough to forget she was there. Bunny was gonna leave the party, just not with Bo behind the wheel. Nossir. Bunny might have been stupid enough to come to the party with Bo, but she wasn't stupid enough to leave with him.

She decided to cut herself off at one mojito, even though her nerves were shrilling for another one. She needed to keep a cool head.

Bunny dodged through clumps of party-goers. There. Chet Martin and his wife. She made for them.

"Why, hey, Bunny!" said Sondra Martin. Sondra had been a year behind Bunny and Chet in high school. "Thanks for that lipstick. That's great stuff. Where can I get some more of that?"

"I'm just about to put it up for sale, Sondra," said Bunny, "but next time I'm over at the office signing Chet's paperwork, I'll leave you another sample."

The three of them smiled at each other.

Bunny waited a beat. "Y'all planning to stay at the party long?"

"We'll probably be heading back pretty soon," said Sondra. "This hard-drinking crowd's not really our scene."

"Look." These were high school friends. She didn't need to mince words with them. "I came here with Bo, but he is already drunk as cooter brown. I'll be scared to get back on the highway with him."

Chet's eyes went wide. "Oh, gosh, Bunny. Ride back with us."

"Y'all are a godsend," said Bunny, with fervor. Bunny wondered if she should tell Mr. Nesbit thanks before she left. It was only good manners to do it, but she thought maybe that was a bad idea. Maybe he'd try to persuade her to stay, and she'd have to be direct with him and tell him no. But he might not notice she'd left early. He was busy with all his important guests. Bo might be too drunk to notice, too. She hoped to god he wouldn't.

Inspiration struck. She'd go back to the veranda and make the polite goodbyes to Mrs. Nesbit. Bo's mother was already in the bag. She probably wouldn't even notice. Probably wouldn't even remember who Bunny was. Then Bunny could check the politeness box and get out of there.

"I'll be right back," Bunny told the Martins.

"Okay, we'll head to the cars," said Chet. Everyone had parked up and down the beach on a flat part of hard sand strewn with sea oats. "Meet you there."

Bunny figured she had plenty of time. The Martins would have to give their key to the valet and wait for their car to be maneuvered out of the pack.

She skirted the picnic and took a roundabout way to the veranda, up some side stairs from the beach. At the top, a covered walkway led all the way around to the front of the house, and Mrs. Nesbit.

As she stepped under the overhang, a burly shape slouching against the wall loomed out of the shadows. "Sneaking off, Bunny?"

Gaaah. Bo.

He was on her before she could scream. He had one hand over her mouth. Shit. This was not Bo's usual handsy stuff. This might be turning into something bad. Bunny fended off the word *rape* as it floated into mind.

Instead, she took action. She bit down hard on Bo's palm.

"Ow," said Bo, grabbing her harder. "Bitch."

She turned smartly into him with a sharp elbow, the way the YWCA women's self-defense class had taught her, six or so years back. She hoped she remembered the move. She tried to get a knee up to nail him in the you-know-whatsits.

"Hah," said Bo, pulling her tightly to him, where she could feel all too well what he thought he was going to do to her. "Bitch."

As they struggled, they inched closer and closer to the edge of the walkway where the dune dropped sharply away from the big house.

Bo lurched at her. He overbalanced. They went over together with a whoop.

Bunny scuttled out from under Bo. He rolled ass over teakettle down the dune, drunk as a boiled owl. He went bouncing and barreling straight into the midst of the party, a fullback-sized unguided missile, a bowling ball through the pins. Ladies in floppy hats and floral flouncy dresses scattered with shrieks of terror, and men in plaid and pink and lime-green pants and plaid and pink and lime-green blazers juggled their drinks to keep from spilling.

"Well, I'll be," said Bunny, scrambling to her feet to survey the carnage. She didn't wait around to see more. She clambered back onto the boards of the walkway and took the long way around the house, heading for the parked cars.

Thank the lord. The Martins stood waiting for her. Their mouths dropped open when they saw the state Bunny was in.

Bunny looked down at herself, biting her lip. Her favorite dress. Bo must've grabbed it by the neck, and when they went off the walkway, he pretty near ripped it clean off her. The whole bodice dangled in ruins. She pulled up the tatters to hide her bra.

"What in the land's sake," murmured Sondra.

"It's that Bo," Chet said, his mouth a grim, thin line. "Drunk as a lord."

"I got away from him." That's about all Bunny could manage. "Now he's the life of the party."

The screaming and fussing came to them distinctly over the beach night noises and ocean sounds.

"Let's get you home, Miss Bunny," said Chet.

"I'll stay with you a while, Bunny," said Sondra, as they neared her house.

"No, but I thank you kindly. I'll be fine."

"Bunny," said Chet, looking over into the back seat, where she sat shaking. Not at all fine. "Want me to call the chief?"

"No police," she said.

"I saw you talking to Charlie Pounder," said Sondra. "He's a lawyer. I bet if you call him, he can give you some advice. Want me to find his number for you?"

"He gave me his card. That's a good idea, Sondra. I may just do that," said Bunny.

She had no intention of calling Charlie about some sordid attempted rape. She did feel inside her purse to make sure she had kept Charlie's card, though.

When she stumbled into her house, the first thing she did was take Bingo out for a quick walk, looking over her shoulder the whole time. It was okay. Bingo was with her. No one would mess with her while Bingo was there. And also, Bo was drunker than who shot John. He wouldn't be able to stand up, much less come after her.

Just the same, when her doorbell buzzed the next morning as she was pouring herself a cup of coffee and trying to decide whether to go to the Lipstick Lab, trying to decide whether she was enough over the shakes to do it, she jumped like someone had stabbed her.

When she opened the door, she like to have to pick her jaw up off the porch. "Mrs. Nesbit. Come in."

Bo's mother sidled into the front hall. She stared around. "This place is different," she said.

"It's because of my parrot. Would you like a cup of coffee?"

"Yes, thank you, I believe I'll have a cup," said Mrs. Nesbit.

Bunny showed her into the kitchen and brought a mug for her to the café table. Mrs. Nesbit no doubt expected Bunny would hand her a delicate teacup, something in a Spode or Royal Doulton.

Mrs. Nesbit examined the mug with interest. *Proud Parrot Mom*, it read. "Now, Bunny," Mrs. Nesbit began. "I guess we had quite a ruckus at the picnic, and I guess Bo's to blame for it."

"Yes, ma'am," said Bunny.

"I hear Bo did not exhibit gentlemanly behavior toward you, Bunny."

"No, ma'am."

"Now, Bo's real sorry."

Then where is he? Can't he do his own apologizing? Bunny thought. But right after, *Keep away from me, Bo!*

"Franklin and I hope you won't press charges," Mrs. Nesbit said straight out, no more beating around the bush.

Bunny got the message. Press charges, and goodbye to Franklin Nesbit's help. But Bunny saw it now. Mr. Nesbit's "help" was nothing but a bribe to get her to help him in a last-ditch effort to straighten Bo out.

"You know—" Bunny summoned up some compassion. This woman was Bo's mother. She must be frightened for Bo. "Bo needs a lot of help." Hell, the Nesbit "help" was gonna disappear on her, no matter what she did. She might as well say what was on her mind. "I'm real mad at what he did, Mrs. Nesbit."

"Sometimes Bo just gets a little bit rambunctious, Bunny. He sees a pretty girl, someone like you, and he—well, he'd be forgiven for thinking that—"

"That what, Mrs. Nesbit?" Bunny leaned forward, fixing her with an eye.

She gave a false little laugh. "Oh, Bo's a good-timing boy, and you're a good-timing girl, Bunny. Now, admit it."

Bunny stood. "Mrs. Nesbit, please leave my house."

Mrs. Nesbit stood, too, patting her mouth with Bunny's napkin. "Well, bless your heart, Bunny. You know I'm right. Fooling around with every delivery driver and grocery clerk from here to kingdom come. Well, after all, with a mother like yours. . ."

Bunny was floored. A low blow, bringing her mother into it.

"Don't go pressing charges, now." Mrs. Nesbit stalked out of Bunny's house.

Why am I the one to feel humiliated? Bunny wondered. *Bo's the one at fault here. Mrs. Nesbit, why, she just threatened me. And Mr. Nesbit sent her to do it. Do his dirty work for him, just like he was gonna send me to do his dirty work with Bo.*

How dare the woman bring Bunny's mother into it? Bunny's father had run off when Bunny was just a baby. Bunny's mother had turned to drink, and then one rainy night, her car had skidded off the road, and. . .

Bunny had been raised by her Great-Aunt Fanny.

But what a hypocrite, Mrs. Nesbit throwing her mother's drinking into Bunny's face. She'd bet money Mrs. Nesbit ticked all the boxes on the alcoholic checklist, and Bo sure as hell did. If Bo wasn't careful, and wasn't lucky, he'd go the same way Bunny's mother had gone. And Bunny didn't intend to be in Bo's stick of butter fancy-ass vehicle when he did it.

When Mr. Nesbit's lawyer called a few days later, the one in charge of the paperwork for the Lipstick Lab, Bunny let it go to voicemail. In the message, the lawyer made a lot of hemming and hawing about how the paperwork had hit some kind of snag. Bunny blocked the number on her phone.

She thought about getting her own lawyer, or going to the police. But she didn't think she had the evidence to charge Bo with anything. Sure, the Martins had seen the state she was in, and they knew it was Bo. Hell, everyone knew it was Bo. But try to prove that. Her word against his, in a court Franklin Nesbit controlled behind the scenes.

All she'd get would be pushed around and labeled—what was Mrs. Nesbit's phrase?—a good-timing girl.

Oh, who was she kidding?

A ho.

Course, Bunny knew most of the town wouldn't believe any such thing. She was friends with most of the town.

She talked it out with Fran.

"Oh, god, Bunny. Bo has taken a dangerous turn. Guess I always thought he was kind of a harmless buffoon. But you're talking about attempted rape. Maybe you should go to the police."

"What would they do?"

"Nothing." Fran sat looking at her hands, then she had folded Bunny in her arms and cried on her. "What a horrible experience!"

Bunny couldn't cry, though. "You'd think I would cry," she told Fran. "I'm scared. And I'm mad. Those are my two emotions."

"You think Bo will have the nerve to come by and try anything with you? After what he did?"

"No." Bunny shook her head. "I don't think he will. I think he'll just let his richer-than-god parents pooper-scoop all his shit up, the way they always have, and just keep on being Bo."

"I do wish I'd been a fly on the wall of that fancy beach Mc-Mansion when Bo came tumbling down the dune into the Nesbit annual party."

Bunny and Fran broke down and laughed. Not very much. Not very hard.

"And he ruined my favorite dress, the d-bag."

"I wonder if you should call a lawyer," Fran said.

"Funny, Sondra Martin said the same thing. Did I tell you I ran into Charlie Pounder at that beach party?"

"Charlie Pounder," said Fran, looking thoughtful. "That's a good idea."

"I don't think I want to lawyer up over this," said Bunny.

She felt embarrassed as she said it. Since when had Bunny Dowdy ever backed away from a fight? She felt miserable and small. She didn't want to do fight that fight. She just wanted it to go away.

"Maybe keep in touch with Charlie, just in case," said Fran, giving Bunny another hug. Then she tilted her head. "How is Charlie, anyway?"

"Fine. Looking good."

"I hear he has done very well. Divorced now, I think."

"Yep, so they say."

"Hmm," said Fran.

Bunny laughed. "I don't need a man," she said. "That's the last thing I need."

"You always need a man, girlfriend," said Fran, pretending to smile. "And you are missing the one you had."

"I'm missing Finn, that's true," said Bunny. "Not a whole lot I can do about that."

When she left Fran's house in Elizabeth City for the drive back to Currituck Cove, Bunny peered through the windshield of the hotpinkmobile.

Life kind of sucked.

Looked to her like she was about to lose her start-up. *And I've already lost Finn*, a little voice inside her insisted. That pesky voice. She wished it would stfu.

Judging from how swollen the low black clouds were, and how greenish the air had turned, it looked like it was about to storm, too.

On the radio, the National Weather Service confirmed it. Hurricane Janelle was bearing down on North Carolina's Outer Banks, and Currituck Cove was right there in her path.

Hurricane Janelle was a force unto herself. She didn't need any men. She backed down from no one.

Bunny had a lot of sympathy for Hurricane Janelle. *Wish that were me. Just me, my own force of nature, no man in it.*

Hurricane Bunny. It had a nice ring to it.

Face time

BUNNY'S PHONE INSISTED on it. Facetime with Finn. Bunny hated Facetiming Finn. A Facetime with him was worse than a phone call. Phone calls were inadequate, but Facetime—actually seeing him on the other side of that screen—was a horrible reminder that the actual Finn wasn't there. In her arms. In her bed.

Finn knew that. But here came that irritating little pinging and ponging sound, so Bunny pressed the button to answer.

"Bunny. I know you hate Facetime. But I had to see you. I had to see you're okay."

"Aww, Finn, we all rode out the hurricane. It didn't do too bad a number on Currituck Cove. Hatteras Island's a wreck, though."

"How's your house?"

"No real damage. A little. Nothing that can't be fixed. Bingo hated the whole thing."

"Ha. I'll bet he did. What about Saz?"

"I think Saz must have been some pirate's parrot, before he took up with me. He got through the storm just fine. He practically yo ho hoed about it."

"I was worried, Bunny. That looked like a really big storm."

"Happens all the time around here." Bunny shrugged. "I'm okay."

"You don't look okay."

"I am. I'm fine, Finn."

"You're not. I can tell."

Bunny was determined not to say a thing about the Bo inci-
dent. It would just worry Finn, and he wouldn't be able to do a
thing about it.

"So. We've gotten clear that I'm fine, Bingo's fine, Saz is fine,
and the house is fine. What about you, Finn? What's going on with
the job?"

"It's kind of frustrating. I got the job. Then the start date kept
getting shoved back. Something about a reorganization of their
management structure. That's why I didn't email you about it. I
kept waiting for the rug to be pulled out from under me. But no.
It's a go, I'm really hired, it's just that I don't start yet."

"Sounds complicated."

"It is, but there's a silver lining. I know I have at least two weeks
before I actually have to be at work. So I thought I'd come back to
Currituck Cove to get the rest of my stuff and not have Sarabeth
Uship it after all."

"Finn!" Bunny screeched. "That's the best news ever!" Eh. The
best news ever would be Finn coming back and never leaving. But
if two weeks is what she got, two weeks is what she'd take.

"Okay to temporarily move back onto my cot?"

"Not okay." They grinned at each other through the frustrating
little window of the screen. "You'll move into my house, you big
jerk. Back into my bed. Wait'll I tell Bingo and Saz!"

Silver linings. People were right. No dark cloud but has its silver lining. The nice thing about Hurricane Janelle was the storm
doing not enough damage to devastate Currituck Cove, but just
enough damage to take local minds off the gossip du jour. The gossip about Bunny and what Bo might or might not have done to her.
That gossip, juicier than most, would have had a long half-life in the

sleepy environment of Currituck Cove. Because of the hurricane, the Bunny and Bo Show was quickly overshadowed.

News as stale as last week's edition of *The Currituck Cove Nickel Shopper*, which Bunny was now smoothing over the bottom of Sazarac's cage.

"Thanks, Janelle," Bunny whispered.

"Good birrrrrd," Saz remarked. Then "Wherrrrrre's Finn?"

"Soon, Saz. Soon, boy."

Later that night, after a trip to the Norfolk airport, Bunny lay curled up beside Finn's long body in her bed. *Where it belongs*, she told herself fiercely. He rolled over to cup her ass in one hand.

It fit there so nicely. Bunny sighed with pleasure.

"God, I've missed this," he said.

"Haven't met many sexy ladies yet in Minnesota, huh?"

"Okay. Let me be clear." He leaned down and kissed her. "Missed you. YOU, not some random sexy lady. This sexy lady, right here in my arms."

"But you know." Bunny looked away. "In two weeks, your job starts. And then." She swallowed hard. "Then you need to move on. We both do."

"Don't wanna." His voice was gruff.

"This long-distance crap. It never works out," she said.

"Sometimes it does. In the academic world, it does."

"In my world, it doesn't," she said. She needed to be honest with him. They both had to face facts.

They agreed to set the whole thing aside, though, and just enjoy their two weeks together.

"And while I'm here, Bunny, I'm gonna spend time at the Lipstick Lab and help you out."

"Okay, cause, well, I've done some research, and you know what the top seller in cosmetics is, right?"

"Yep. Lipstick. You told me that."

"But the top DOLLARS don't come from lipstick. They come from eye products. So I'm thinking of adding an eyeshadow line, and that's a very different consistency. I've fooled around with it a bit, but—" Bunny bit her lip.

"You can't get the consistency right."

"You know me well, Finn."

"But here I am, to save the day. Mighty Finn is on his way."

She giggled.

In the morning, he swung into his old place in the Lipstick Lab like he'd never left it.

At the morning break, Florella/Brenda popped in with Krispy Kreme. "It's a welcome-back-Finn present," she said. She had one Krispy Kreme in hand already, chocolate with pink and green sprinkles. She took a mammoth bite.

"But Brenda—uh, Florella. It's not vegan," Bunny began.

"Umm, well, Krispy Kreme is its own food group, you know?"

"Florella, you fraud. Hand em over," said Finn.

Bunny fired up the Keurig machine and found enough clean mugs. Brenda's own inspiring mug for her, Bunny's Heisenberg mug for herself, and a mug she'd gotten for Finn, one that read, **Scientists are just regular people** and then, in tiny type, *who are way smarter than you*. Brenda and Finn opened the Krispy Kreme sack and found a clean place to spread out the bounty.

As Bunny fussed with the Keurig, she heard them talking.

"So, guess all that Bo shit has died down," said Brenda.

Bunny whirled around at the same time Finn was saying, "What Bo shit?"

"Ooops," said Brenda.

"It's nothing," said Bunny, directing a dirty look at Brenda. She handed the coffee mugs around. "Just some jerk who got drunk and a little handsy."

"Someone put his hands on you?" Finn's voice was ominous.

"It was stupid," said Bunny. She bit into a Krispy Kreme. Filled strawberry.

"Mr. and Mrs. Nesbit shipped Bo off to Pine Manor Estates," said Brenda.

"Good. Dry him out. Maybe it will help." Bunny made herself look placid and unconcerned. Underneath, she was going *Yes!!!!* Bo was off somewhere. She'd never been able to shake the idea he lurked around every corner. Silly. I mean, he hadn't hurt her. *He tried to,* that voice inside told her. *He may try again.* "Pine Manor Estates. They say it has a great rehab program."

"As if this isn't his third or fourth trip up there," said Brenda, munching. "Okay, welcome back, Finn. See y'all around." She pushed her chair back and waltzed out of the place.

"Okay, Bunny. Time to come clean. Think I haven't noticed how nervous you are? Think I haven't noticed how nervous Bingo is, for fuck's sake." Finn swiveled around to face her.

"You heard Brenda. Bo is gone now."

"Okay, who is this Bo character, and what did he do, exactly?" He put a finger under her chin and tilted it up so he could look her in the eye.

So then Bunny had to tell him.

At the end of it, Finn was steaming. "Go to the cops."

"I can't," she said. "They won't do anything. I mean, I could, but all it would accomplish is getting everyone's tongues wagging again."

"Look, Bunny. What he did. That's beyond handsy. It sounds dangerous."

"I know," she quavered, ashamed she was sounding so weak. Now he'd worry himself sick when the time came for him to leave. And she wanted him to leave happy and confident she'd be okay, even though their relationship couldn't continue.

Course— She had to face it. *I'll be a wreck. But he doesn't need to know that.*

"Look," she said. "I know a lawyer, a very good lawyer, no one beholden to Mr. Nesbit or anyone in his crony crowd. Someone up in Raleigh. If I start to feel threatened, I promise I'll call him, okay?"

"Okay," said Finn, seemingly reassured.

Later that night, as Bunny slipped into bed, Finn took more than his usual nanosecond in the bathroom.

"What's going on in there?" she called from the bed.

"You'll see."

He appeared in the bedroom doorway, silhouetted by the light from the hall.

Bunny let out a shriek.

"Got you a little something after my first paycheck," he said. "Forgot about this last night. Meant to put it on first thing."

"Come here, you."

The tighty-whiteys were gone. Finn posed in the sexiest guy underwear Bunny had ever seen. And she had seen her share.

"These things, I mean, I didn't know a respectable department store sold something like this. Had to hide them from my mom."

She yanked him down on top of her.

"I'm gonna have to move out of my parents' house. My mom is, like, pretty nosy."

"Are we really going to talk about your mother at a time like this?" Bunny demanded.

"No. How about talking about this instead." He guided her hand where he wanted it to be.

"How about not talking?" she said.

And that was just the second night.

The two of them banished any gloomy thoughts so they could make the most of their time together. Bunny had a lot of satisfying talks with Finn about parrots, about lipstick, about everything. And a lot of more than satisfying times that didn't involve any talk at all, beyond moaning each other's names and whispering in each other's ears and ripping off each other's sexy underwear as quickly as humanly possible.

They did talk over Bunny's business dilemma. "I'm going to lose this little start-up," she said. By then, she'd told him about the whole fiasco with Mr. Nesbit and how it connected to the Bo fiasco. "And now that's over. Mr. Nesbit thought he could buy me, but no, no he couldn't."

"Nobody can buy you, Bunny," said Finn., leaning over for a kiss.

"I had a real flare of hope, though," Bunny told him, after the kiss and its aftermath were over. "But I told you before, putting a good product in front of customers takes a whole lot more than the good product by its own self. It takes all kinds of marketing, and that takes all kinds of cash."

"Cash you don't have."

"Yeah. Your rent payment before you left tided me over, and then I had a real hope that an infusion of cash from Mr. Nesbit would make the difference. Now that's gone."

"Any ideas?" Finn took her hand and stroked it. They were sitting at one of the long tables in the Lipstick Factory, and Bunny had just finished squealing over the perfect smooth-on cream eyeshadow Finn had whipped up.

"One, maybe," she said. "I'm thinking that if I can scrape up the money to go a major cosmetics trade show and exhibit my samples, I may be able to attract interest from some big company. They could buy me out, or bring me into their organization. I wouldn't just love that. I want to be my own boss and run my own outfit. But I'd take a deal like that rather than go under."

"Show me," Finn said, swiveling her laptop around so they could look at it together. "Where's the next one of these trade shows?"

"There's the big one in Las Vegas. That would be expensive to get to. But look at this one." Bunny tapped some keys. A web site popped up on the screen. "Here's one in Atlanta, not as big but pretty big. I think a very small rented booth might not be out of reach for me, and I could drive there."

"Wow, Bunny. Let me check something." He took over the keyboard and tapped in a web address of his own. "Wouldja look at that. The same weekend. A big agribusiness conference."

"At a university?" She looked dubious.

"Yeah, see, I could write a paper to deliver there, or a poster for a poster session. I could get my company to pay for travel. One of their recruiting points was a fund for their scientists to present at conferences. I could be down there when you are, and we could build in time before and after our events. We could have five or six days together. Close to a week. If I can get the conference hotel paid for, you can stay in my room."

So when Bunny took Finn back to the airport with two huge boxes of his stuff, she didn't feel so sad. If this worked out, they'd see each other in only a few months.

But as she drove home from Norfolk, the gloom descended again.

She and Fran had coffee that week, and Bunny told her all about it. "It will be great, if it happens. But Fran. You know what? This is just putting off the inevitable. We both know we need to move on, tell each other goodbye."

"But neither of you can do it," said Fran softly.

"We have to. I need to see Finn sitting across from me at the breakfast table. I need to see his face in the morning, when I wake up and turn over and there he is beside me in my bed."

"Something may work out. You don't know," said Fran.

"Aww, Fran. Maybe it will. I'm betting it won't."

Key takeaway

BUNNY BEAMED AT FINN from the far side of the huge expanse of yet another hotel king-sized bed. "We did it!"

"The planets aligned." He beamed back at her. "Your trade show, my poster session. The only problem, I want to leap on you right here, right now. Instead, I gotta get prepared."

"I know." Bunny felt gloomy.

"This isn't a bad thing," said Finn. "My poster session is on the schedule first thing, so I'll get it over with, and then we'll have the whole weekend to play."

Bunny knew that wasn't exactly the truth. Finn would have a lot of networking to do, if he was to get the most out of his conference. Maybe a contact leading to a more satisfying job, maybe in someplace like Timbuktu or farthest Antarctica.

She sat quietly on the bed, listening to the gargling and shaving noises coming from the bathroom. When Finn emerged, he was resplendent. His tan suit was nicely pressed and he looked suitably scientific. She had given him a present, a bright blue tie with little green parrots woven all over, and he was wearing it.

"Uh," she said. "I'm glad you like the tie, but is it the right—"

"You don't understand about scientists, do you? It's perfect for this. Maybe not stockbrokers or bankers. . ." He trailed off, his eyes cutting to himself in the mirror above the dresser as he fiddled with the knot.

"Let me," said Bunny. She retied the tie in expert fashion.

He grabbed up his portfolio and was out the door.

"Good luck," she called after him.

She spent the morning at the rental booth in the conference center next door to Finn's own conference hotel. Her booth was pretty basic, but she had dressed it up nicely with a great display of her products: the three lipsticks, the two eye shadows, and professionally designed brochures and business cards. No one needed to know that Gina the professional designer was her best friend, right? In a crystal bowl, tiny pots of lipstick samples. In another, the eyeshadows.

A buyer strolled by and stopped. Bunny smiled at her, holding up the lipsticks bowl.

"Tell me about these," said the buyer.

"Bernice Dowdy." Bunny handed the buyer her card. A logo graced the card, the booth, the brochures. The Lipstick Goddess, read the text, with a stylized image of Sazarac looking mighty pleased with himself.

"This is Hot Bunny Pink," Bunny said, pressing a sample on the buyer. "This is Like a Boss Red." Another sample. "Here's our third, Sazarac. All organic, vegan-friendly ingredients. And our mascot—" Here she tapped Sazarac's image—"demands one important thing from us: no animal testing."

The buyer looked down at the third sample, enchanted. "What a rich color," she breathed. "Love the parrot."

"We do, too." Bunny smiled.

"Love the ethical angle!" the buyer cooed.

Bunny smiled bigger. "Good ethics is good business."

By the end of the morning, Bunny's smile was feeling a little ragged. But that was because she was smiling so much her face hurt. Her products were a hit. She headed back to the hotel room to refill her sample bowls.

She hadn't had time for breakfast. Coffee—that necessity—she gulped from cardboard cups she grabbed from the counter in the conference center's entryway.

At the hotel, she freshened up and flipped open her laptop in hopes of at least one or two orders. She began to smile harder. Two orders, both from well-known stores, for several cases each of all three colors of lipstick, and the eyeshadows, besides.

Bunny's heart did a little backflip. She was already thinking hard. Here was the problem with success. To fill these orders, she'd need a lot more space, a more streamlined assembly process. She'd have to hire mixers and fulfillment workers. So the problem became—could she afford success? She'd have to, even if it meant mortgaging the beach house.

And then—her finger paused on the list of incoming emails and scrolled down.

Wow. Bunny caught her breath.

An offer from one of the big brands to buy her out.

A lot of success, really fast. Bunny sat down on the side of the bed, a bit dizzy. Of course taking the big outfit's offer was the most sensible of the paths. She'd gone in knowing something like that would be practically irresistible. She wouldn't have to mortgage her house or hire anyone. Just license the lipstick names and formulae to the company, maybe even her logo, then rake in the cash. Who wouldn't want to go that path?

But the other path—she'd have to invest, and take risks. In the end, the whole enterprise would be hers and hers alone. After her franchise fiasco, something about that appealed to her mightily.

She decided to go back to her booth after lunch, keep pushing her samples, and see whether any other orders came in. Then she'd have to make some tough decisions.

But before she did. . . Her stomach growled. Lunch. She and Finn had plans for the end of the day. Not for lunch. She was on her own for that. As she headed over to the chic little hotel restaurant recommended for casual lunchers, she put her own gratifying successes out of mind and sent up a plea to the universe for Finn: *please let Finn's poster session go over well!* He was probably just finishing up with it now.

Poster session. Her mind drew a blank. She realized she hadn't asked Finn enough questions about what a "poster session" was. She'd had vague ideas of fifth grade, and the science fair, and that classmate of hers who had turned in a crayoned poster showing a cross-section of a baseball.

Her own project wasn't much better. A potato clock. Aunt Fanny had gotten the idea from it out of the back of a magazine, alongside ads for sea monkeys and liniment. She and Bunny had gotten a big spud from the Piggly Wiggly and made the thing together. It was fun. It was ugly. It didn't win any prizes.

Aunt Fanny. Up in that Raleigh nursing home. Bunny felt bad. She hadn't been making enough time to go up there and see her. Not recently. She determined to send Aunt Fanny a letter as soon as she got home. Aunt Fanny didn't do email. She had loads of friends up there. Her friend Edna, for example. Aunt Fanny's letters were all full of Edna this and Edna that. Lately, Aunt Fanny hadn't mentioned Edna. That worried Bunny a little. All of Aunt Fanny's friends were old and frail. Every so often, one of the friends died, and then Aunt Fanny got down in the dumps.

Bunny shook off the guilty thoughts. She'd write, and she'd plan a visit, as soon as she got home.

On a whim, she detoured away from the corridor leading to the restaurant, and down the corridor leading to the exhibits. Finn might still be there! She could use some cheering up. Funny to feel down when success was staring her right in the face, but it was true. She did feel a little down. Besides, she wanted to find out more about Finn's own interests.

He wasn't in the exhibition hall. No one was, except for a few knots of people talking together quietly in front of a few of the booths. Everyone else had gone off to lunch, most of them to a big welcome banquet advertised on all the conference center's digital reader boards. Finn was probably at the banquet. Free food, right?

Bunny browsed among the exhibits. Some of the posters were pretty basic. Others were impressive, looking like professional graphics people might have designed them. They all had big headlines proclaiming *Background, Methods, Results, Key Takeaways.*

"I'm so self-centered," Bunny whispered. "I've been so focused on me and my exhibit and my products and my marketing—me me me me me—that I haven't asked Finn too many questions about his exhibit." Her whisper was eerily loud in the huge echoing space. She looked around quickly. Suppose someone overheard her, the crazy cosmetics lady, in this austere space? Talking to herself?

She wandered to the front of the room and ran her finger down a long directory. There. *Johansen, Finn.* Row E, exhibit 32A.

Soon Bunny was standing in front of Finn's poster.

She gasped.

There, bigger than life, was a blow-up photo of Sazerac. Her eyes moved to the title of Finn's exhibit: "Computer simulations in pesticide toxicology testing: Humane alternative to testing on animals." Beside the title, his name. And three other names. Wow, Finn had collaborators.

Bunny cast her eyes rapidly over the text on the poster, and all the graphs. A lot of it was gobbledygook to her, but one paragraph really stood out, the one labeled *Key Takeaways*:

> We ask the question why, with sophisticated computer tools available, corporations and laboratories would test on animals. In the U.S., many lab animals fall outside the USDA's Animal Welfare Act applying to test subjects such as dogs, cats, and monkeys. The act doesn't cover animals such as rats, mice, birds, fish, and reptiles. Some of these animals are quite intelligent—budgerigars, for example. We show that three easily obtainable off-the-shelf computer tools can effectively substitute for testing on animals like these, and without the ethical complications of animal testing. These computer tools are just as economically feasible as testing on purpose-bred animal populations, and more feasible than testing on free-living animals, with comparable or in many cases better and more accurate results.

Bunny leaned closer to the display and read the paragraph again. The graphs and the math parts and all the stuff about computer models might be hard for an ordinary person to figure out.

But this part. This part Bunny got. She zeroed in on a word. *Budgerigars*. Science language for parakeets.

She remembered Finn using that word.

Don't test on parrots! Don't do it!

She found she was getting emotional, and over this dry scientific language, too. She laughed at herself.

But she marveled at Finn. He was turning his firing into an asset. He was taking his convictions to a big scientific meeting like this one, and doing research with other scientists to show he was right.

Bunny felt proud.

The thing about restaurant seating

WOW, THOUGHT BUNNY as she made her way thoughtfully back to the restaurant area of their hotel, attached to the conference center. Finn seemed so much a part of her life—a photo of Saz as the focus of his exhibit—but so far away from her, too. It made her head hurt, trying to figure it out.

She did try. Finn was a person who lived in a world she could barely imagine, one with these other people who swarmed through the conference center stuffed with ideas and data and knowledge. Finn could have conversations with all of them about stuff like science. He couldn't have those kinds of conversations with her.

It's not all about making conversation, she told herself with a giggle, visualizing Finn's lush mouth, practically feeling it on hers. And his hands on her. And other parts of him on her. In her. By the time Bunny got to the little lunch restaurant, she was getting hot and bothered.

But as the waitress ushered her to a booth and she sagged into it, the thought kept gnawing at her. What she and Finn had together was not all about conversation, true. But not all about sex, either. Something else lay beneath both. Something deeper.

Still. *Finn and me, we're wrong for each other*, that little voice kept telling her.

Looking at the menu cheered her up. This was a good hotel, and the restaurant lunch choices looked pretty delicious. The waitress came over to take her order.

When the restaurant hostess ushered a couple into the booth just beside hers, Bunny barely noticed. She was trying to figure out how to switch from dwelling on her gloomy thoughts. She worked on moving her mind instead to the fun thoughts.

Lunch. That was one. Two was much more important. What she hoped to do with Finn when they reunited later tonight. What she hoped he'd do with her. She thought of his new sexy underwear and began to smile.

Service was swift. The waitress came back with Bunny's salad and iced tea right away, a little packet of artificial sweetener on the side. Bunny grinned. Gonna glow in the dark for you tonight, Finn! She eyed her salad appreciatively. Shrimp, avocado. Mmmm. She picked up her fork.

She pricked up her ears.

The voice from the booth that backed up to hers. She gasped. Finn's voice.

She was on the point of bouncing up and sticking her head out of her own booth when a cautionary something stopped her. The patented Bunny Intuition.

Another voice came from the booth next to hers. A woman's voice. A cool, cultivated, educated voice.

"Listen, Finn. Let's get our lunch, and then let's talk. So much has gone on between us. We have a lot to process."

To process, thought Bunny, her mouth hanging open. Then she relaxed. This must be a business conversation or—she didn't know—some kind of sciency conversation. That did it for Bunny. No way she was going to pop into the middle of a conversation like that. Somebody might be scoping Finn out for a job. *A lot to process.* Bunny's mind ran immediately to making sausage. Or cosmetics. No. Probably some fascinating science process.

In the next moment, the Bunny Intuition kicked in big-time. She leaned back to hear better. No science involved, or not essentially. No cosmetics involved. The process was about sausage. Definitely sausage.

Finn said something she didn't catch. Bunny was shamelessly eavesdropping now. Finn sounded growly and definitely kind of angry.

Bunny picked at her salad.

The waitress hustled past Bunny on her way to Finn's booth. Finn's and that woman's. Bunny's own waitress was their waitress, too. She was carrying a tray with their lunches on it, and the two in the booth backing up to Bunny's were silent as the waitress said nice things and distributed the food.

There was a silence.

"I don't know why I'm here." That was Finn. "I don't want anything to do with you, Rona. I told myself I wouldn't have anything to do with you."

Lordy. The woman with Finn was Rona. Finn and Rona. Like a Boss Red Rona.

Bunny had a conscience-pang. She should make herself known. It was wrong to keep listening in. She kept listening, feeling guilty. But not a lot. Not enough to stop doing it.

Decades of overhearing gossip in the booths at The Mermaid back in Currituck Cove kicked in. Her eavesdropping skills were honed. They were matchless. Bunny kept listening.

"It's just lunch, Finn." Rona's cool voice again. "Not like I'm tying you down in my hotel room. All I ask is that you hear me out."

There was a long pause, punctuated by the noise of silverware clinking against plates.

"Okay," said Finn at last. "You've got my attention. Say what you're going to say."

"I know what happened to you, after. . ." Here Rona hesitated, her ice-queen façade dropping maybe a teensy bit. ". . .after you and I ended—"

"Just say it," Finn growled.

"It must have seemed harsh."

An incredulous snort from Finn.

Yeah, baby, Bunny said to him in her mind. *Don't take any shit from that lady.* But another little voice said, *So, why did he agree to have lunch with her?*

"It was necessary, Finn." The ice-queen voice was back. "It was business."

"So. Business is all zero-sum. You win. I lose. You get a promotion, I get the axe. And into the bargain, I get my career ruined."

"Hamilton gave me an ultimatum. What we had was special, Finn. Finn, would you stop the eye-rolling for just one minute and listen to me? Hamilton had me by the balls."

Bunny nearly did a spit-take. Rona had balls? Well, maybe she did, at that.

"And now you're a vice-president. Thanks, Hamilton," said Finn.

"Except I'm not."

"You're not?" Finn's voice changed from angry with a hefty shot of sarcasm to jaw-dropped-on-the-table amazed.

"I was. Hamilton did make me V.P. Then I resigned. Just last week."

"Why."

"New opportunity. And Finn, I want you to be part of it."

"You're joking."

"I'm not."

"After what you did to me, you want me to follow you to this new opportunity of yours?"

"Finn, Finn, Finn. Are you really this naïve? You're a scientist. So am I. And I'm a woman of business into the bargain. What do personal feelings have to do with it?"

Everything, Bunny mouthed fiercely.

"Everything tasting good?" The waitress stood beside her, friendly and smiling, refilling Bunny's water glass.

Bunny managed a numb wave of the hand.

Back to listening in. There was a pause.

That waitress is refilling their water glasses, too, Bunny realized.

"Well, here we are," said Rona finally. "You're here, I'm here, we're eating lunch. You may as well listen to me while I describe the opportunity. Then you tell me you don't want in."

Bunny wanted to haul around to the other side of the booth and smack the confidence right out of the woman. She sounded so sure Finn was going to sit there and listen to her babbling on and on about her opportunity. *Get up and walk away, Finn*, Bunny sent to him with all her patented Bunny Mind-Power.

Finn didn't. He sat and listened.

"You know what we talked about," said Rona. "We always talked about a better way of doing our jobs. Your idea about using computer modeling instead of animal testing. Your know-how about what to model. And my computer chops. The perfect marriage."

Bunny winced at the word *marriage*.

"And then, instead of standing up for our idea, making a case for it, you caved to Hamilton." Finn's voice was low and vicious, but Bunny made out every word, because he enunciated every one.

"Hamilton had found out about us." Rona's own voice was matter-of-fact.

"We had something, Rona. Or I thought we did."

Bunny wanted to cry, the hurt coming through Finn's words was so clear. So much pain.

"Don't tell yourself fairytales, sweetheart."

On the spot, the name for Bunny's new black-mauve lipstick color shot into her mind: Ice-Queen.

"So," said Rona after a long pause. "The opportunity is this. I'm starting my own company. I have the backing." A slithering sound.

No, Bunny decided, not Rona slithering out of their booth like the serpent she was. Papers being pushed across a table.

"You can read those. Take them to your lawyer. It's all there. It's all legitimate and solid. And you were right. Computer modeling is the future, and animal testing is getting a bad odor. This company of mine will make its bones on that change in the zeitgeist. Big agribusiness needs a way to look good, and this is a way it can do so in the eyes of the public. I'd be stupid to ignore that. And Finn. I'm not stupid. As for you."

Another pause. The ice-queen voice thawed a bit. "You haven't just crawled into a cave to lick your wounds like I thought you would, Finn. Mister Too-Sensitive Finn. Mister Animal Lover. I can admit it. I was wrong about that. I can tell from your poster session. You're working on this, working hard. You have solid ideas, not just daydreams, the way I once thought you did. I want you on my team. How does Vice-President for Research sound to you, Finn?"

"Didn't I mean anything to you? I mean, personally?" Finn's voice sounded kind of strangled.

Rona's low laugh penetrated to Bunny, skulking in her own booth. "You have great abs, Finn. You're a great kisser." Her voice dropped, but Bunny heard. "You're the total package, if you know what I mean."

Another long silence. Bunny sank down into her booth in agony. She felt herself begin to tear up. *No*, she told herself sternly. *Don't.* Not here, anyhow.

"Check, please." Rona's voice.

It seemed an eternity before the waitress came back with their check. An eternity before the rustling from the other booth let Bunny know Finn and Rona were about to stand up and make their exit.

Thank the good Lord, Bunny prayed—and it was a real prayer of thanks, too, a patented Bunny Plea to the Higher Powers—that Bunny's booth was toward the far side of the room and theirs was closer to the exit. They wouldn't have to pass Bunny, shaken and about to lose it, as they left the restaurant. But then, she knew that. She hadn't seen them come in, and they hadn't known she was right behind them, listening to every word.

The tears began to leak down Bunny's cheeks. *Lucky that mascara's waterproof,* she thought disconsolately. *And the eye-shadow Finn made me.*

The leakage turned into a flood.

"Aww, honey." It was the waitress, standing by her, shielding her from any other diners who might walk by. She handed Bunny a tissue.

"Thanks," Bunny hiccupped.

"Men," said the waitress with a knowing look. "They're not worth it, honey."

The waitress brought her some coffee with the hotel logo stenciled on the mug, so she'd have time to get herself together.

Once Bunny managed to do that, she paid the waitress, leaving her a big tip for emotional support services. She slunk from the restaurant and headed fast for the hotel room, where she could fall apart in private.

Her feelings for Finn brought her low, and so did her guilt. She felt so low-down she could crawl under a snake's belly. Eavesdropping like that, it was real trailer park.

But as much as Bunny beat herself up, as much as she knew it was her own fault for being nosy and underhanded, she couldn't stop the pain.

It was real clear. Finn still had feelings for Rona. Rona had hurt him, and he still hurt over what she did to him. Did Finn hurt when he had to leave Bunny and the beach? Maybe. But not like he hurt over Rona.

That's the trouble with these booths in restaurants, she told herself, flinging herself onto the king-sized bed. Sure, you score a lot of gossip, lurking in one of those things. But stuff you didn't bargain for might get dumped right down on your eavesdropping trailer trash head.

Withdrawal syndrome

BETWEEN THE TIME BUNNY got the wreck of herself back to the hotel room and the time Finn breezed in to get ready for dinner, Bunny had made some decisions.

Would she confront Finn with what she knew? Never.

Would she let him know how much he was hurting her? Never.

Of course, he may not take Rona's bait, she thought. But she had a suspicion he would. It was exactly what he was looking for. A responsible position at a socially responsible company. A way to make a difference. A way to practice his science skills and get paid—Bunny didn't know this for certain, but she figured—paid a lot for doing it.

It took Bunny a while to get in shape for Finn's return. To shore up her nerves, she bought a pumpkin spice latte from the Starbucks in the hotel lobby and took the signature cup back upstairs with her to a soothing bubble bath. She completely repaired her hair and makeup. By the time Finn came in from his day, she looked like a knockout. She knew she did. In some nasty part of herself, she wanted him to eat his heart out.

As Finn shut the hotel room door behind him, he let out a long, low whistle. "Maybe we could postpone dinner," he choked out.

"Aww, Finn, I'm so sorry about this, sweetie, but I can't go to dinner. I have this killer opportunity with a big company. They want to buy me out. I'm going out to dinner with the CEO," she improvised.

His face fell. But he said, "Wow, Bunny. That's great. I guess? Didn't you want to run your own outfit?"

"Yes, I did," she said, passing the big company's paperwork over to him. She had printed it out at the hotel's business center. "But when you get an offer this sweet? Well, you'd be a fool to pass it up, just because you had some silly dream, wouldn't you? This is business, Finn. It's not about personal feelings." She smiled at him. And if her smile wasn't sweet as sugar, but only between two hundred and maybe a thousand times sweeter the way artificial sweetener was supposed to be that much sweeter than sugar, well, then. She'd take her chances and glow in the dark later, if she had to. A big, wide artificial smile, with a thin line of acid underneath, sharp and lethal.

He blanched. Didn't say anything. He took the paperwork she handed him and swiftly passed his eyes over it. "Looks like a great deal for you, Bunny. You'll end up well-off, looks like. They'll franchise your name and products, and you'll get steady income from it. I agree. Get the paperwork checked out by a lawyer, then go for it."

He turned to the dresser and began unknotting his parrot tie.

"What about you?" she said. "Did you have a good day? I hope yours was as good as mine. I meant to come by and have a look at your poster, but I'm afraid I couldn't find the time. Maybe tomorrow."

"I'll have to take it down in the morning," he murmured.

"Too bad. I have meetings all morning. Maybe you can tell me all about your poster sometime," she purred. "All those results and outcomes and key takeaways. All those charts and graphs. Not that I'd understand a thing about it."

"I hate it when you get into that airhead act of yours, Bunny," said Finn. Not like he was angry. Like it made him sad.

She ignored his remark. "Did you uncover any good opportunities for yourself? I hope you did."

"One," he said, dropping his parrot tie on top of the dresser. "Maybe."

"Hope it's as good as mine."

"Maybe," he said again.

"Of course, cosmetics is all about making people feel great about themselves, and what you do is all science and math and stuff. Guess there's not much comparison."

"Maybe not."

She scooped her purse from the bed and headed to the door. "I may be late, so don't wait up," she said over her shoulder. She had the hotel concierge call her a cab, and then she took herself to Phipps Plaza, to a tiny out of the way mall restaurant, and forced herself to down a big steak dinner, flipping off the one guy who tried out some cheesy pickup line on her.

"Girl's gotta keep her strength up," she said to herself, as she made herself take a last bite. She ordered a couple of drinks to go along with the food. But she cut herself off so she wouldn't cry into her drink like some pathetic over-the-hill cougar lady. Come to think about it, maybe that's exactly what she was.

To kill the time after dinner, she strolled down the mall to a travel agency still open for late shoppers, and grabbed a fistful of brochures. One for Paris. One for New Orleans.

Bunny decided if she couldn't have Finn—and now she saw it, she couldn't, they were too different and he was still in love with Rona—she'd have fun instead. Her go-to strategy.

Because he was. He was still in love with Rona. She'd heard it when she heard the hurt in his voice.

Who could love that cold bitch? Finn, apparently. And Bunny was a fool, not being able to see that. If there's one thing Bunny Dowdy couldn't stand, it was acting like a fool.

Tomorrow, she'd head back to Currituck Cove to find a lawyer and do her due diligence with the contract. She'd sign The Lipstick Goddess over to the people prepared to pay her a tidy sum to get it, she'd close up her little cosmetics factory behind the UPackWeDeliver, and she'd travel while she thought about next steps.

Next steps in her quest to have fun, fun, and more fun.

She went to a movie in the mall's theater. Later, she couldn't even remember the title. Some silly rom-com. She cried through a lot of it. Before the credits rolled, though, she pulled herself together so her eyes wouldn't look puffy. During the movie, she decided she was addicted to Finn, and she had to break that addiction. If that mean withdrawal symptoms, painful ones, the shakes and stuff—well, that's just what it would take.

The price she had to pay for letting herself. . .in the dark, she made herself say it. *Fall in love.*

Not a good look on Bunny Dowdy. Not a good look at all.

When she let herself quietly into the hotel room, it was late. The room was dark. A shaft of moonlight showed a big hump in the covers.

Finn.

Bunny swallowed hard. Lucky for her Finn slept like the dead. With the minimum of fuss and noise, she got herself ready for bed, then slid into the covers on her side of the big king-sized bed, staying as far away from him as possible.

"It's for your own good," she whispered to herself. Then, looking over at Finn, "and yours."

Finn flipped over, moaning a little.

He's dreaming, she realized. In the moonlight, she let her eyes linger over his face, its planes, the lashes longer than a man had any right to. The lips.

Those lips.

She longed to run her finger along them. And her tongue, too. With a moan of her own, she turned her back and tried to sleep.

She didn't sleep much. It didn't take much for her to wake early and be in the shower as Finn started to stir.

She came out wrapped in a towel, grabbed her clothes, and popped back into the bathroom.

When she emerged after a good twenty minutes, fully clothed, completely made up, Finn made a surge for the bathroom, muttering good-naturedly about cosmetics and what it took to apply the darn things.

He came out five minutes later freshly showered. No towel.

He sat down on the bed, and she handed him a flimsy cardboard cup of hotel coffee-machine coffee. She looked away.

"Not tempted, huh? Hoped you would be." He took a sip. Made a face. He stared back up at her with his green, green eyes. "What's going on, Bunny."

"Early morning," she said, falsely cheerful. "Gotta meet with my backers in fifteen minutes." She reached for her purse and put her own coffee cup down.

"Bunny. Tell me."

"Tell you what?" She didn't look at him. Breaking up with a naked Finn. It didn't feel right. All her instincts told her to pounce on him instead. But breaking up was not only the right thing to do. It was the only thing to do, and she knew it. She had to do it.

"Something's wrong."

"Look. Finn. This has been fun. What we've had, it's been real fun. I've enjoyed every minute of it." The whole thing marched out of her mouth like a rehearsed speech, but she hadn't rehearsed anything. The words just kept on coming. "You have to go back to Minnesota. I have to go back to North Carolina. It's just the way things are, nobody's fault."

"Are you breaking up with me, Bunny Dowdy?"

She blinked back tears. No time for that. Besides, she had shed too many of them in the past twenty-four hours. "Yes. I'm afraid I am, darlin. That's the only sensible thing to do, and you and I, why, we know it, don't we? We're big boys and girls here. We have to face facts. The two of us, we come from different worlds, and now we actually live in different worlds. It's just not working for me, and I'm guessing it's not working for you, either."

"Don't put words in my—" he began. Then he went quiet. "I see."

"I'm driving back early," she said. "I need to see a lawyer about this contract, and I know a good one in Raleigh. You stay here and enjoy the hotel, though."

His face darkened. "I'll be sure to do that," he bit out. "Now that you've gotten your success, playtime's over, huh? Time to put the toys away."

"Oh, don't go being like that. Don't spoil what we had. It was great." She got out of the door without breaking down, and walked as fast as she could to the bank of elevators. Thankfully, at least nine or ten people had congregated there, so if Finn had come after her.

. .

Breaking up with a naked man. That's the way to do it. Then they can't come charging down a hotel corridor after you.

And he didn't.

And that's that, she told herself.

Withdrawal. It was just as painful as everyone said it would be. More painful than Paris. Much more. *Silly me, I'm not even sure why*, she thought. Etienne had had a glamor about him. Finn was just a nerd in hot pants.

A hot nerd in hot pants, she reminded herself. Then she had to face herself. A whole lot more than a hot nerd in hot pants. A tender lover. A loving man. A man who believed in something. Damn. But it was right to leave like this, while she wasn't shattered into tiny pieces, and she knew she had done the right thing.

Shutting it down

"WELCOME BACK!" A FAMILIAR figure eased through the open door of The Lipstick Factory. Florella/Brenda, bearing a bag of Krispy Kreme.

"Hey, Brenda. Florella," Bunny amended. She was worn out. And here came Brenda—Florella—to get on her last nerve.

Florella/Brenda waved the bag of Krispy Kreme under Bunny's nose.

"Got any of the Glazed Chocolate Cake?"

"You know it, girlfriend," said F/B. She handed over the bag.

"Mmm," said Bunny. "Thanks, Florella." *Make an effort*, she scolded herself. *Brenda wants to be Florella, let her be Florella.*

"How was the trade show? I should get myself a booth at one of those. How about I pick your brain?"

"It was good. I got an offer from a big company. They'll buy me out."

"Aww. Thought you wanted to be your own boss. Oh, how was—" B/F nudged Bunny and wiggled her eyebrows. "—Mr. Hotpants?"

Damn, thought Bunny with irritation. That was her own private name for Finn. How dare Brenda? "He's good."

"Is he coming here any time soon? Bet you're missing him."

"Brenda. . ." Bunny had to take a big gulp of air. "We broke up."

"Aww."

"Yeah."

"Feeling bad?" B/F produced a little cake of soap, as if by magic, and thrust it into Bunny's hands.

"Thanks."

"That's sad, Bunny. He was great. And he really liked the lipstick stuff. And he really likes your parrot."

"Yeah."

"These long-distance things." B/F shrugged. "They never work out."

"Nope," said Bunny. "Well. I have to shut all this down." She waved her hands around vaguely.

"You're really doing it. You're really selling out and letting someone else have The Lipstick Factory."

"Looks like it. Guess I'll take inventory in here—but I still have to get a lawyer to look over the paperwork."

B/F glanced at Bunny sidelong. "A lawyer from around here?"

"No," said Bunny, with more force than she intended. "I don't trust any of these good old boys."

"Smart. You were always the smart one, Bunny. Of our whole bunch, you were the smart one."

"Me?" Bunny raised an eyebrow. "I didn't even make it through community college."

"You have other smarts."

"Anyway, I do know a smart lawyer, and so do you."

B/F cocked her head at Bunny.

"Charlie Pounder."

"Charlie fucking Pounder!" B/F crowed. "Yes! You're right, he's a smart guy. The smartest. I remember him. The one they had to find a special calculus teacher for. The one who made a 5 on the AP history exam. And he's a lawyer, they say, some big muckety-muck up in Raleigh. He'd be pretty expensive, though, Bunny."

"Yeah. I'm guessing he doesn't take on small potatoes stuff like my little business, either. But he gave me his card at that beach party—"

"THAT beach party," B/F said, nodding sagely.

"—and told me to call him, so I guess I will. Then he can steer me to some lawyer who deals with this stuff."

"Good move," B/F approved. "Divorced now, too, I hear." She looked at Bunny carefully.

"Shut up, Brenda. Any more of the Glazed Chocolate Cake?"

B/F peered into the bag. "No, but there's a dee-lish Strawberry Iced With Sprinkles, and it's calling your name." B/F lifted the bag to her ear. "Buunnnneeeeee...."

"Give it here, you fruitloop."

They grinned at each other and sat around a while longer, eating Krispy Kreme and drinking coffees from Bunny's Keurig machine.

The next day, Bunny called Charlie.

"Come on up to Raleigh," he said. "We can have a nice dinner together, you can tell me about your business, informal, all that, and then I can steer you to a reasonable lawyer, if that looks to be necessary."

So Bunny headed to Raleigh a few days later. A great idea, because then, after she saw Charlie, she could pay her Aunt Fanny the visit she had promised herself she'd make. For months she'd promised it and had never followed through. That needed to change. If anyone was a special presence in her life, Aunt Fanny was.

Bunny made herself economize on the hotel. Not a Patented Bunny Move. But things had to change, and change hurt. Sure, she might be right on the cusp of financial success, but she didn't know that. Better to be prudent. Besides. . .

Bunny looked around at the rather beige room. No Finn to share it with. Even the fanciest hotel room would feel barren with no Finn in it.

She slumped down on the queen-sized bed.

Then she made herself freshen up. She put on one of her prettiest dresses and did one of her most expert makeup numbers on her face, with all her own products and a little boost from Mélisande.

When she came down to the hotel lobby to greet Charlie, she felt distinctly better. Charlie looked great in his very expensive tailored suit. They went out to eat at a trendy Raleigh restaurant, New American cuisine, craft cocktails. Bliss.

Charlie's all-American boyish good looks were very attractive, too. Bunny's man-radar was pinging.

"This business of yours sounds great, Bunny," Charlie told her over dessert. "And the opportunity with the big company sounds like a very practical move. There's a lawyer in my firm, Amanda Fernandez, who specializes in stuff like this. Let me set something up with her. I'm guessing she'll be open to meeting with you as early as tomorrow. Can you stay around?"

"Let me call my pet-sitter," said Bunny. She'd planned to make a quick visit to Aunt Fanny, then get on the road back to Currituck Cove. But with this appointment, she'd stay the extra day.

"You always were a dog-lover, Bunny. Didn't your Aunt Fanny have that great black lab?"

"Yeah, and now I have my own. Bingo." Bunny flashed a proud-owner phone pic of Bingo. "But I also have—" She found she needed to take a sip of liquid courage before going on. "—a parrot. A Senegal." And she flashed that pic.

"A parrot. Wow, Bunny. I didn't figure you for a parrot kind of a lady."

"Me neither, but then Sazarac just got me." She tapped her chest. "Right here. Shot to the heart."

Charlie beamed at her. The waitress came for the check, and he reached for it.

Bunny did a quick mental calculation. The check must have been eyebrow-scorching high. Charlie didn't bat an eye as he handed the waiter his credit card.

"My treat," he said. His eyes softened. "Sazarac. And you ordered one." He pointed to her empty drink.

"Yeah. Named my favorite parrot after my favorite cocktail."

Somehow, it seemed like a violation. Drinking a Sazarac, and talking about Saz, to anyone but Finn.

But Finn was over. Absolutely, definitely over. Bunny had made sure of that, and if she'd had any doubts, the next day's meeting with Amanda Fernandez proved it.

The next morning, as she sat on the side of the hotel bed—empty hotel bed, no Finn in it—she thought about everything she needed to bring to Ms. Fernandez, and everything she needed to get clear.

One of those things was Finn.

It had never occurred to her before now.

What obligation did she have to Finn, anyway? If not for Finn and his chemical chops, she'd never have been able to create her lipsticks and eyeshadows.

"But we had no legal agreement," she explained carefully to Ms. Fernandez, during their meeting. "He was just a friend who happened to know a lot about chemistry, and he helped me out."

"I see," she said. "You know, if you go into business with a friend, it's best to spell these things out—"

"Oh. No. We weren't in business together. He was just helping me out."

"Not an employee?"

"No."

"I don't see that you have any obligation to him at all, then," she said. "Not legally. If there's paperwork, even an email, between you, something about how he's providing his expertise to you—"

"No, nothing like that."

"I think you're in the clear. It's possible he could sue, but I doubt he would. Especially once he saw how hard it would be to make a case for it, and how much money it would cost him to do that."

"But—" Bunny bit her lip. "The thing is, I feel like he should get something for his part in making the products a success."

"A moral obligation," Ms. Fernandez said carefully.

"Yeah, that's it. A moral obligation."

"It's up to you if you want to make some kind of legal provision for Mr. Johansen. I wouldn't advise it. But if you want to do it. Well, maybe get in touch with him, and—"

"That's just it. I can't seem to get in touch with him." Bunny sank down on her Herman Miller miserably. In the waiting area, she'd tried to text Finn. The little red i told her, *Not delivered.* Then she had tried to call. Repeatedly, the call went straight to voicemail, with no call back. Bunny had realized then. There would never be a call back, because Finn was never gonna get the voicemail. "Finn has blocked me," she whispered.

"What's his address?"

"Do you know how many Johansens there are in the Minneapolis phone book?"

To her credit, Ms. Fernandez didn't make Bunny feel stupid. "You don't know his address?" Her tone was matter-of-fact.

"No, he moved to Minneapolis, and we just communicated by phone, but something seems to be blocking my messages. . ."

Ms. Fernandez waited, her eyes sympathetic.

"I think he might actually live in a suburb of Minneapolis, or his parents do. Apple something. Apple Grove? Apple. . ."

Ms. Fernandez tapped on her computer. "Apple Valley?"

"That's it!"

A moment later. "There appear to be quite a few Johansens in Apple Valley. Do you know his parents' first names?"

"Uh. No."

"Ms. Dowdy, I know you want to help Mr. Johansen out, do the right thing and all, but I can't see how you'll do that, and you have no legal obligation to do so. I'd leave it alone."

Her voice betrayed more than a lawyer's meaning. She saw through Bunny right away. This was a broken heart kind of a thing, not a lawyer kind of a thing.

Bunny nodded, feeling numb.

"Aside from that, the agreement the company has sent you looks fine for the most part. I'd suggest changes here—" Ms. Fernandez tapped on the paperwork spread out between them. "And here. And here. I'll have a revised copy typed up, you can fax it to them, and we'll see what they say. I'm guessing they'll go for it. These changes are to your advantage, but they're nothing at all unreasonable."

"Thanks, Ms. Fernandez."

"Amanda," she said with a smile. They both stood and shook hands.

By the next day, it was a done deal. The Lipstick Factory no longer belonged to Bunny, and soon she'd be reaping the financial rewards.

She composed a long email to Finn and sent it. She didn't get a reply. She didn't expect one.

For a month, Bunny was on the big company's payroll while she wound things up in the little space behind the UPWD and shipped everything they specified to the new owners. Sarabeth the teenager UPWD clerk helped her with that. The company even agreed to buy out the last months of Bunny's lease through Chet Martin.

Nice and tidy.

Bunny's bank account was fat and soon to get fatter.

So why did she feel so down?

At least the visit to Aunt Fanny in Raleigh had cheered her up some. Aunt Fanny might be old, but she saw straight through Bunny.

After the hugs and kisses and small talk in the nursing home's nice lounge, Aunt Fanny reached a frail liver-spotted hand to Bunny's and patted it. "Man trouble."

"I went and got my heart broken," Bunny confessed.

"The worst kind of man trouble, some say. But Bunny—" Aunt Fanny paused and stared over the tops of her trifocals into Bunny's face. "I'd say the worst kind is just flitting like a butterfly from man to man, and using that to keep yourself from any real feelings."

"But then, the real feelings get real painful," said Bunny, tearing up.

Aunt Fanny handed over a lace-trimmed hankie.

They both paused while one of the nice aides wheeled a jiggling cart over to them and offered them coffee in little crystal clear cups. Balancing the cup and saucer on her lap gave Bunny something to do. A way to turn the conversation to different things. To Aunt Fanny, and how she was doing.

Now it was Aunt Fanny's turn to tear up. "I sure am missing Edna," she said.

"Where'd she go?" Bunny was dumbstruck.

"You don't know? I suppose I wondered, when you didn't answer my letter. Poor Edna. Her heart just gave right out, honey. Oh, maybe six months back. She didn't suffer. So that was a blessing."

"Aunt Fanny! I've been a terrible niece!" Six months, thought Bunny with a guilty start. That's how long she'd been out of touch with Aunt Fanny. But there was the Finn thing, and the start-up, and the Bo thing, and the hurricane, and—Bunny thought about the whole experience of attending the Raleigh science conference with Finn and not thinking once about visiting Aunt Fanny. Stuff like that had to change. Bunny's fantasy of Aunt Fanny surrounded by friends was fraying. The friends were getting old and dropping off the branch like autumn leaves. Aunt Fanny would live forever—Bunny was sure of it. But she'd be getting lonelier and lonelier.

"You're a wonderful niece," said Aunt Fanny.

"I never got the letter about Edna. Oh, I'm so sorry, Aunt Fanny. Do you think you could have the nice aides here help you set up an email account? It's really easy. We could keep in touch better that way."

"I'm too old for that, dear," said Aunt Fanny.

Bunny knew that look. Old-school Aunt Fanny and her letter-writing, the letters on scented lavender monogrammed stationery. Case closed.

"Anyway," said Bunny brightly, before she rose to go, "I think I'll be spending more time up here in Raleigh, so I'll visit more often. That's a promise." At Aunt Fanny's inquiring look, Bunny went on. "I met a man up here. Well, actually, I guess I renewed an acquaintance with an old high school friend who moved up here. Charlie Pounder. You remember him."

"The smart one. Yes. That sounds promising," said Aunt Fanny. "Best medicine for a broken heart. Move right on."

"But not flit around like a butterfly." Bunny's laugh was rueful.

As she drove back home, she wasn't so sure about that. All those feelings for Finn. She kept trying to shut them down. It wasn't working. The Finn longings kept bursting back out.

And her go-to method for avoiding heartache? The Patented Bunny Fling? Maybe that wasn't working as well as it used to. As well as she hoped it might.

Putting a Band-Aid^{tm} on it

ADA THE PET SITTER and Bingo greeted Bunny's return from a whirlwind New Orleans trip, Ada with a smile, Bingo with bounding enthusiasm. Saz was more subdued.

"I think—" Ada began, leading Bunny to Saz's cage. "Can parrots get depressed? He seems a little down."

Once Bunny was unpacking and alone in the house, she didn't go out to The Mermaid for lunch, as she'd planned. She stayed home for special Saz time. Ada was right. Saz wasn't his usual self. He screamed a lot. He was plucking.

"Saz," said Bunny, worried. "You've never been a plucker."

"Wherrrre's Finn?" said Saz.

"Oh," said Bunny, surprising herself by bursting into tears. She quickly got a handle on her feelings. And here she had been so sure she was over Finn. So over.

Now she wanted desperately to text him and have him text back. At the very least, ask him what Saz's behavior could mean.

But really, Bunny was pretty sure she knew. Saz was missing Finn as much as she was. Somehow, even with Finn's absences over the past months, his reappearances had seemed to give Saz the boost he needed.

Now Finn was gone. Really gone. Somehow, Saz knew it.

"Guess there's a vet visit in your future, Saz," Bunny said to him, offering him a sliver of honeydew melon. Watermelon season was long over. "I need to make sure something's not wrong with you physically," she explained to him. She wondered if there were parrot psychologists.

Saz picked at the piece of melon indifferently.

Bingo whined.

"You know Finn's gone too, don't you, Bingo?" said Bunny, leaning down to pet him. "Well, guys. Expect a nice change. There's a new man in my life. Wait'll you meet him. His name's Charlie."

Saz and Bingo didn't look convinced.

New Orleans had been a blast. Bunny had reconnected with the fun guy she had met down there the year before. They had gone dancing. Bar-hopped. Bunny tried new cocktails. She did not order a sazarac. She and Mr. Fun New Orleans Guy had lingered at romantic breakfasts in the French Quarter over beignets and coffee with chicory.

By the time Bunny got off the plane in Norfolk, she was more than ready to go home, though. The fun all rang hollow. Mr. Fun New Orleans Guy was right out of the Bunny Fling cookie-cutter mold, and—she saw to her horror—that mold no longer satisfied.

"Thanks, Finn," Bunny whispered, half meaning it and half wishing she'd never fallen for him and let him ruin other guys for her.

Maybe not all guys.

Right there in the airport as she deplaned, Bunny got a satisfying little burst of warmth. She opened an email from Charlie: "I'll be in town next week to see about my dad. Let's have dinner!"

Bunny made up her mind. She had to move on. And here Charlie was, a lovely man. He was nice to look at, he was rich, he was rich AND decent, unlike the Nesbits of the world. Smart. And he really liked her. Finn was not the only smart guy in the world who really liked her. Who saw past the airhead.

Bunny decided she owed it to herself to see where the Charlie thing might go. What it might lead to.

Dinner at the nice steakhouse in Elizabeth City went well, when Charlie came to town. It was one of the only two "fine dining" establishments in the area.

Charlie's mom had died years ago, and now he was in the process of moving his father up to Raleigh. His dad was a pretty lonely old guy whom Bunny never saw around town any more.

"He needs people around him," Charlie told Bunny over dinner. Charlie had a sister, but she was a decade younger and had moved to Little Rock. She rarely visited.

Such a pleasant time! One thing led to another. Bunny invited Charlie back to her house, where he admired Bingo and Saz. He wasn't a real animal lover. Bunny saw that right away. And he had an amused glint in his eye as he looked over Bunny's house, turned into its own mini-animal refuge.

But Charlie was a good kisser, and eventually they ended up in Bunny's bed.

When Charlie left to go back early the next morning, he had gotten Bunny to agree to a long weekend at his place in Raleigh. He insisted she not make breakfast for him before he left. They enjoyed coffee in bed, and then he kissed her and headed out.

Bunny threw on jeans, a tee, a sweater—it had gotten chilly—and took Bingo on his morning walk. "Good thing I have you to get me up and going, Bingo," she told him. "Otherwise I'd lay around in bed half the morning."

When she got back, she forced herself to eat a piece of toast. And then, darned if she didn't go back to bed.

"I'm a lady of leisure now," she said to Bingo. "I'm entitled." She had officially declared herself early-retired. All she had to do was cash her checks from the company that had licensed her cosmetics. She didn't need to do any more work than that, to live a comfortable life.

But lying around in bed all morning wasn't just lady-of-leisure stuff. Something else was going on, something she had rarely ever experienced. *Maybe I have Saz's disease*, she thought moodily, staring out the window and listening to the soothing sound of the surf.

Sex with Charlie. That had been nice.

"Sex" and "nice." Did they belong in the same sentence?

The sinking feeling in the pit of Bunny's stomach grew. She was ruined for sex now. Finn had ruined her.

Still and all. She had to move on. Had to move past Finn. Had to. Bunny wiped away a tear. Stop that! she told herself.

She genuinely liked Charlie, and so she was looking forward to the weekend with him. He was great company.

The weekend was as good as Bunny thought it might be. On Friday night when she arrived, Charlie took her to a great restaurant—another one! On Saturday, he whipped up a gourmet breakfast for them both and served her breakfast in bed.

That afternoon, they went to the North Carolina Museum of Art, which was having a special exhibit of contemporary artists.

"My friend Gina should be here," Bunny told Charlie as they browsed through the collection together. "She's the one who knows about art. I don't go to many museums." Only one, in fact, on a high school field trip. She wasn't about to admit that to Charlie.

"What do you think of these?" Charlie waved his arm around.

Bunny stepped up to a mammoth piece taking up an entire wall. She found herself kind of fascinated. The colors. The texture of the paint, applied in thick brush strokes. Unconsciously, she stepped back to take in the whole piece, and then laughed at herself. She was behaving just like a cartoon museum-goer, or the ones in movies. *But you just naturally step back*, she told herself. *Otherwise you can't see the total effect. You just naturally stand staring, because the experience is so overwhelming.*

"So?" Charlie raised a quizzical eyebrow.

"I think this one is my favorite."

"Why?"

"Oh, Charlie. You know me. I'm not very sophisticated. You know that." Bunny passed off her awkwardness with a laugh.

"Bullshit," said Charlie. "Don't think about whether you're sophisticated or not sophisticated or any of that b.s. Tell me what you see."

"Well, I'm looking at that big shape there. See how it kind of connects with that line down there? And those colors!"

"You're a natural, Bunny," said Charlie. "Perfectly understandable. Anyone with a good fashion sense, like yours, and a great sense of color—" He reached out and lightly touched her lips with the tip of a finger. She was wearing Ice-Queen today.

"You have a nice way with a compliment, Charlie. That could turn a girl's head."

"I'm not flattering you. It's just true."

"Uh huh." Bunny grinned at Charlie, and he grinned back. Bunny had fun. That night, yet another great restaurant meal, all of it making the best of Elizabeth City look shabby.

And Charlie's house. It was magnificent, beautiful wood and marble and lush upholstery and huge windows letting in shafts of sunlight.

"Sharon did it all," he confessed with a grimace.

"The ex."

"Yeah. It's okay. We get along okay. Our divorce was for the best, and we didn't have kids, so there's one huge complication we didn't have to face."

"Nice. No nasty ex. I'd say that speaks well of you, Charlie. You and your ex still being friends."

Charlie laughed a bit uneasily.

On Sunday morning, they were lounging around Charlie's rec room, wet bar in the corner, a nice grouping of leather furniture around a big slab of a rough-finished granite-topped coffee table. The coffee table was strewn with magazines, mostly business publications and a few sports magazines.

"Hang on. I'm going to make you a great espresso." Charlie slung himself off the leather sofa Bunny had sunk into so deeply she figured she'd never be able to haul herself out again. Soft leather, butter-soft, not the stiff hard shiny stuff.

She did manage to scramble forward. She leaned over to pick up one of the magazines, a Raleigh business magazine featuring the leading lights in the local and regional business community.

Bunny's hand paused mid-pickup.

She felt a chill, the way you would if you thought you were reaching for something completely innocent and suddenly realized what you had in your hand was a rattlesnake.

There, smiling from the cover, Rona Petreius. *Tech start-up blazes a new trail.*

"Here you go, ma'am." Charlie was back with two tiny elegant cups.

Bunny carefully put the magazine down. She picked up her cup and took a sip. "Mmm."

"Good, huh? I love that machine. Bought it for myself last Christmas."

"Hey, Charlie. Do you know her?" Bunny nodded at the magazine.

"Rona? Sure. Everyone knows Rona. She is a mover and shaker around here. That article's about her new company. Seems to be taking off, too."

Bunny tilted her head, taking Rona in. Those lips. That lipstick was too pale. Bunny wanted to send Rona some Like a Boss Red. She sighed at herself. She always wanted to send Rona some Like a Boss Red.

Then a thought struck her.

Of course.

Rona's company was based in the Research Triangle. Right here in the Raleigh/Durham area.

And that meant.

Bunny gulped.

Finn. Rona's new Vice-President for Research, isn't that what Rona had called the position she'd dangled at Finn over lunch? That meant Finn would be in Raleigh too. He wouldn't be in Minnesota at all. He'd be here.

Bunny grabbed the magazine and paged directly to the article about Rona and her start-up. She scanned the article. The lead article in the journal. The cover article. *Dr. Rona Petreius is on her way to yet another success in her string of tech successes. . .* Rona was hot stuff. She didn't just look good. She wasn't just smart. Dr. Rona! She was a force. How did Bunny think she could ever compete with that?

"You're interested in this kind of stuff?" Charlie picked up the magazine after she set it down.

"Women running their own companies? Sure," said Bunny.

"That could have been you," said Charlie. "Sorry you sold out?"

"That would never be me." Bunny put the magazine down and tapped Rona lightly on the face. No mention of Finn in the article, that she could see. The article was Rona all the way. That's the way she likes it, Bunny realized. It has to be all about her.

"No?" said Charlie.

"No. This is serious stuff. I'm a start-up goddess, too, but just a goddess of cosmetics."

Charlie guffawed.

"I'm glad I sold out. With the income I'm taking from that deal, I'm officially retired. Just gonna have fun."

Charlie gave her another sidelong look. "Bet that's not going to last long, Bunny."

"What do you mean?"

"I mean I've never met a woman with so much energy. I'm guessing you won't stay officially retired long."

Bunny laughed.

"So are you interested in these techhie things?" he persisted.

"Not really. I'm interested in—" Bunny was about to make something plausible up, and suddenly she realized she didn't have to, because it was the truth. "—interested in animal welfare. I read up on that, all the time." That was kind of a stretch. But she resolved, then and there, that she would turn it into the truth. She'd find journals. She'd do computer searches. "I heard a rumor about this company," she continued, picking up the magazine with Rona on it again. "Rona Petreius's company. Something about using computer models to substitute for animal testing."

"Like in the cosmetics industry," said Charlie.

"That, and other industries. Agribusiness uses animal testing. It's not right."

"You never stop surprising me, Bunny," said Charlie. He took the magazine from her and stared at it, too. "Yeah, Rona's company is all about computer modeling." He leafed through to the article. "Yeah. Business analytics. She'll make a killing."

"Nothing about animal testing?"

He shook his head. "Nope."

"Maybe the rumor is wrong."

"Could be it's right, only the whole thing is just greenwashing. You know."

"Greenwashing? No, I don't know. What's that?"

"It's when a company makes a lot of noise about supporting some worthy cause to get itself creds and publicity in the right circles, but really doesn't intend to do much with the cause. Whatever the cause might be. It's like whitewashing. Only. . .greenwashing, because a lot of times these worthy causes are about the environment, how the company will be good for the environment, that kind of thing."

"Or animals," said Bunny.

"Or animals."

"Hmm," said Bunny. "Just window dressing."

"Pretty much. Greenwashers talk a good game. Then they don't do squat. Or if they do anything, it's some token effort."

Wonder how Finn likes being the token animal lover in Rona's empire, Bunny thought sourly.

Then she got a little scared. Suppose she and Charlie were out to dinner and came face to face with Rona and Finn? Charlie had already revealed he and Rona might operate in the same circles. "Do you have many clients in the tech industry?"

"Tons," said Charlie. "Not Rona, though. She's with a law firm we think of as our top rival."

So I'm right, thought Bunny.

But she didn't have time to obsess over the thought. It was time for her to head home, and as she took the hotpinkmobile east toward the coast, she fervently thanked whatever guardian angel in charge of her that she hadn't turned around at some restaurant or cocktail party to find Finn and Rona staring her down. She couldn't have handled it. Not if she got blindsided.

Now she knew, though.

"Forewarned is forearmed," she said out loud to the landscape speeding by. "Next time I'm back in Raleigh, I'll have my game face on." Finn was never gonna know how much she hurt for him. But she had dumped him, right? And kind of cruelly. So he was the one who deserved to hurt. She didn't.

Why was it she was the one who was hurting most? She was sure she was. Finn was employed with Rona. He was seeing Rona, the woman he clearly loved. The woman he was just made for.

Dr. Finn and Dr. Rona. They were a couple, the perfect tech power couple. If it bothered Finn that he was just window-dressing in Rona's empire, well. Money and prestige had a way of easing that kind of wound. Putting a Band-Aid* on it. Kissing the boo-boo.

Thinking *Finn* and *kissing* in the same sentence. Not a good idea. Bunny made herself concentrate on her driving.

*THE JOHNSON & JOHNSON Company wants you to know that Band-Aid^{tm} is a brand name. There! I've told you!

Gimme shelter

DURING ONE OF BUNNY'S visits to Raleigh, always with a wary eye out for Finn, she brought Saz along in a travel cage. She took him to see an avian veterinarian there.

"I don't see any signs of physical disease," said the vet, Dr. Bekele. "Big changes in his life lately?"

"Yeah."

"Tell me more." Dr. Bekele smiled reassuringly at Bunny. Bunny liked the vet. She was a lovely-looking woman. Ice-Queen would look great against her flawless dark skin.

"Well, Saz came to me in a strange way," Bunny began. She went through the entire Saz saga, and she didn't hold back about Finn. "I'm Saz's favorite human," she said. "I think. At least, if Saz is gonna preen someone, that someone is gonna be me. But he loves Finn, too. And now Finn is gone."

"What a story!" Dr. Bekele laughed. "And you have no idea who sent you this parrot, or why?"

"None."

"So let me see," the vet said. "Clearly, the parrot has had a former owner, but we don't know anything about the circumstances that led to Saz being shipped off to a stranger. Death of the owner, maybe? We don't know. Whatever the circumstances, they could have been pretty traumatic for Saz, even though he—or she—looks to be a well-adjusted bird."

"He," said Bunny.

"Okay, he. But now, he's had another traumatic separation. From your friend Finn."

"More than a friend," Bunny muttered.

"Yes, I see," said Dr. Bekele. "Saz shows all the signs of grieving."

And so do I, thought Bunny. She waved the thought impatiently away. "That makes sense," she said instead.

"I'm glad you brought Saz in. He should have regular checkups to keep him healthy. But in this case, I think you just need to give him extra attention and reassurance. I see the way you two are with each other. I'll bet you're already giving him the loving attention he craves. Just keep doing what you're doing. But it will probably take a while for Saz to get over missing his other friend. Here's something you might consider," she added. "Parrots are very social. Ever think of getting a second bird?"

"Oh," said Bunny. "I'm not sure I could manage two. I have a dog, and—" She thought about it. "But I'm retired, early-retired, so—"

"Think about it," said Dr. Bekele. "A lot of people don't just jump into parrot ownership, you know. That's not your situation, because Saz showed up in your life out of the blue. But look how good you are with him! Still, most people inch up on parrot ownership. They volunteer at a shelter, maybe foster a bird or two. You could maybe look into something like that."

"How do I do that."

"Hmm," the vet said. "You know, I believe there's a parrot rescue down around Edenton. That's kind of far from you, but you might get a lot of ideas from a trip down there. They're not our clients, but I can give you the name and address."

Bunny left a sample of Ice-Queen with the receptionist before she left. "It'll be perfect on your boss," Bunny confided to the woman. "Will you make sure she gets it?"

The receptionist grinned and winked. "Will do."

"And here's something for you, too," said Bunny, slipping her a sample of Hot Bunny Pink.

Later that week, she made time for a drive down the coast to Edenton Parrot Rescue and its crusty owner, a sturdy woman known to everyone as Miss Winnie.

Miss Winnie showed Bunny around.

The rescue boasted a large outdoor aviary. It was buzzing with happy parrots and similar birds. And a few unhappy ones.

"We're working on those. That African Grey. Poor guy, he lost his owner, and he's in mourning. That's a hard adjustment for an African Grey."

"I've heard that," said Bunny. "My bird is having a hard time, too. He's a Senegal, so maybe it's a bit different, but he's still in mourning." She explained Saz's situation to Miss Winnie.

"Fostering a bird might help," said Miss Winnie.

About a month later, Bunny had a second parrot. She didn't name him. He already had a name. Buster. And she was only fostering him until Miss Winnie could find him a good home.

"He needs socializing," Miss Winnie said. "His former owner neglected him and then just abandoned him. So I took him in. He needs a forever home, but before that, he needs some manners."

Saz, Bunny realized after a day or two, had been a very easy bird. Buster was his own feather riot. He was a caique. Miss Winnie taught Bunny how to pronounce it: *kai-eke*. And told her the caique is the clown of the parrot world.

Buster was an evil clown. Luckily he came with his own cage. Bunny kept him in a different room, letting Saz get used to Buster's noisy calls and also observing a quarantine period, although Miss Winnie had assured Bunny a vet had checked Buster out and he was disease-free.

But the day had to come when Bunny needed to introduce him to Saz. Buster immediately tried to establish dominance, and Saz immediately showed Buster who was boss.

Bunny had to separate them and try again several days later, armed with treats as bribes.

She was about ready to throw in the towel with Buster, or at him, but then she reminded herself Buster had had it hard, and Bunny should try to help him get along in a world that didn't feel like a very secure place, not to poor Buster.

By then, Bunny had completely given up on her house and its décor. It belonged to the parrots now.

By the end of the next month, Buster was getting nicely social-ized, enough for Miss Winnie to place him with a new owner.

"Good luck, Buster," Bunny called after him.

Damn. Bunny was becoming a parrot lady. The town's crazy parrot lady. Brenda/Florella confirmed it, arriving on her doorstep the day Bunny brought home her next foster. With a bag of Krispy Kreme, of course.

"Treats for the Parrot Lady," Florella announced.

Bunny couldn't hate her. Because pumpkin spice.

Also, her arrival signaled a Patented Bunny Bolt From the Blue.

Bunny the Parrot Lady. Bunny could object. She could reject that label. Or she could lean in.

Bunny started laughing, even though she could see Florella thought she was a couple ants shy of a picnic. Once she knew what Bunny had in mind, she'd be sure of it.

Start her own parrot shelter!

On a clear, crisp winter day, Bunny assembled her team: Florella, Ada, Fran and her new husband Nelson and her new stepdaughter Deanie, and best of all, Gina and Doug, down from the mountains. They'd brought Bongo with them, so Bingo's joy was complete. Another lab to play with!

Does he realize Bongo is his son? wondered Bunny. Is Bongo shouting in Dog, *Daddy!* Probably not. But look at them frolic! In their doggie way, they knew they were connected.

The team built an aviary in Bunny's spacious back yard. She'd checked with Chet Martin—he'd know about zoning and such. Was she violating any zoning laws?

Nope. Currituck Cove didn't have too many of those.

"To make double sure, you could take the whole thing to the city zoning board," Chet said, stopping by to watch the aviary go up. "But if you do, count on a few sourpusses to try and stop you."

Bunny knew just who he meant. People like that busybody Amelia Gardner, the one who had tried to make trouble for Doug and Gina.

"I'll take my chances. What's the worst that can happen? They'll tell me to take the aviary down. But I'll make it such a success that they won't want to."

At Chet's raised eyebrow, Bunny went on. "Tourist attraction as well as do-gooding. You know that sea turtle rescue down at Topsail? All the beach-goers want a tour through that place. I'll do the same."

"Good thinking," approved Chet.

"I'm already working on some really cute signage," Gina put in, overhearing.

"Mostly, though, this place will be for the parrots," said Bunny. "Saz is gonna love it. He loves flying around the house, but I see the look in his eye when he spots the great outdoors through the window."

"Shouldn't the birds have shade?" said Ada the pet-sitter. "Should we build the aviary under a tree, Miz Dowdy?"

"No, I talked to Miss Winnie about that. Suppose in the next storm a tree limb falls on the enclosure? We don't want that. But the birds do need shade, you're right, Ada. What we want is THIS." She pointed. Doug and Nelson were dragging a big carton in from Nelson's pickup in the driveway. It was a pop-up gazebo.

The friends drove posts to frame up the aviary, and stapled wire mesh, with a wire mesh top so no parrot could take off for the wild blue yonder and get itself lost or hurt. The floor was wire mesh, too, raised off the ground to discourage predators who might try to burrow under. Once the floor was done, the friends covered it with a layer of gravel. The finishing touch—a variety of perches and water bottles. And, of course, plenty of parrot toys.

Throughout the day, Bunny passed around slices of take-out pizza from Mervin and Bob's Pizzeria across from the Pure gas station, and plates of chocolate chip cookies from Suzanne's Bakery, the bright star of Currituck Cove's tiny downtown. Plus Suzanne's really great coffee, doled out into a miscellany of Bunny's mugs through the spout of a take-out carafe.

"Done," said Bunny, hands on hips, looking over their handiwork. "Let's give this aviary a test drive."

She loaded Saz into his carrier and brought him out to the aviary. Saz went crazy in there.

"He loves it!" Bunny grinned at her friends. "Thanks, guys!"

Giving it the Saz Seal of Approval, Saz made satisfying little plops of bird poop all over it.

The friends went out for a big feast at The Mermaid, and the next day, since the winter was turning out mild, Doug got in a round of golf, his passion, at the new golf club where he had once owned a condo. His friend Theo owned it now, but Theo and his partner Len were out of town.

The last thing Gina did, before she and Doug left to go back up to the mountains, was nail up the big sign she had designed: **Sazarac's Place: A Shelter for Parrots and Their Friends.** With a picture of Saz on it.

Was it a little too close to her lipstick line's logo? Bunny narrowed her eyes. No biggie. The company buying her out had completely changed the logo of her product. It was a big pair of lips now.

She sighed every time she moved past her stuff displayed on some department store's cosmetics counter. It was hard to lose control of an enterprise she had nurtured from idea to success, and watch strangers take it in directions she never intended. But she guessed a big pair of lips went better with a name like The Lipstick Goddess.

And she was happy to cash the company's quarterly check.

Because that was funding the parrot shelter, and now the Saz design was all hers again.

Once everyone had cleared out of her back yard. Bunny and Ada roved through the aviary, deciding on what else it needed to become the perfect welcoming place for parrots.

Now for the birds, thought Bunny. Miss Winnie had promised her a few fosters for starters. Birds who had kind of given up on stability. Who were miserable or out of control because of it. Who needed safe shelter while they worked things out and the humans who cared about them worked on their behalf.

Losing control. Finding shelter. Bunny guessed these matters weren't only the stuff of cosmetics and corporations and animal rescue operations.

They were maybe about her, too. About humans and what they experience, and what they need.

Rescue me

THE YEAR CAME AT BUNNY fast. Sazarac's Place was a success. She fostered birds for Miss Winnie, she accepted birds from Dr. Bekele and other avian vets who heard about her, and every so often, an abashed-looking person arrived on her doorstep with a cage or carrier. Someone who was moving because of a job and couldn't take her parrot with her. Someone who was being moved into a nursing home that didn't allow parrots.

"Hmmph," said Aunt Fanny, sitting with a mug of coffee featuring a lunatic stick woman on one side and *Crazy Parrot Lady* on the other. "Our place allows all kinds of small pets. Our place knows they're good for the residents." Poor Aunt Fanny's canaries had long ago died, and she hadn't replaced them, but she still loved birds. Bunny brought her down to Currituck Cove as often as she could, although the time was fast coming when Aunt Fanny wouldn't be mobile enough for that. "Did you know my good friend Edna had a parrot?" she asked Bunny, tearing up.

"No, I didn't know that," said Bunny. "What happened to it?"

"When Edna died, her nephew took it away. I hope he took good care of it. Edna loved that bird. Her name was Pirate Queen. Queenie for short. She was a character! Saz reminds me a lot of her." Aunt Fanny fixed her old eyes on Saz. She didn't see very well any more. "I think Edna's bird might even be the same kind as yours."

Thinking of Edna and her parrot reminded Bunny of the hardest of all rescues for her to smile through—the adult children, grandchildren, friends, friends of friends who showed up with grieving parrots of elderly owners who had died.

Bunny was careful not to accept too many birds. She wanted to make sure she could take care of the ones she had. Any overflow she sent down the coast to Miss Winnie, whose aviary was huge. Even so, by the end of the year, Bunny had added on to hers.

There were a couple of bad moments. Amelia Gardner, town busybody, threatened to make trouble. "All that squawking," she huffed. But Bunny's neighbors actually loved the birds, and they arrived with Bunny at City Hall to make sure the shelter could go on.

And Bunny had been right about parrot appeal to tourists. Once a day, she allowed visitors to take a tour of her aviary, and she had a little talk all prepared—what parrots were like, what they needed, all the fascinating parrot factoids.

Sometimes Bunny got sad, afterward. She knew that not too long ago, she had been a complete parrot novice. Lucky for her Finn had come into her life, right along with Saz.

Sometimes Saz was sad, too. "Wherrrrre's Finn?" he would say in a mournful voice.

At those times, Bunny would make a fresh resolve. Find a fun new fling.

The problem with that, the whole idea of a fun new fling had lost the "fun" part. Now it just felt desperate.

"You should settle down with some nice man," Fran told her once.

Bunny just laughed.

How did I get this dumb? she asked herself. First, I just flit from man to man. Then I find the one man who spoils all the flitting, and then, I dump him. In spite of not wanting anyone else but him.

Dumping him. For Finn's sake, it was the only thing she could have done. She was too old for him, too wrong for him. The woman who fit him had hurt him, but then in a kind of miracle, that woman had reached out to make it right. Finn's very own miracle. She couldn't begrudge him that, not and say she loved him.

Dumping Finn. The right thing. How come it felt so wrong?

Hard work was the cure, and Bunny was a worker. She turned her avian rescue into a success. Her friends helped her out, too, in many ways. She had turned Ada the pet-sitter and waitress at the golf club (and Gina's best high school art student, don't forget that, Bunny reminded herself) into Ada the able animal rescue assistant. If she happened to be out of town, Ada led the tours. Ada was a jewel, and Bunny was thrilled when—with the help of Charlie—Sazarac's Place earned the coveted 501(c)3 tax designation that meant the rescue was a bona-fide nonprofit organization, and could take charitable donations, get grants, and pay salaries. Ada was first on her payroll. Bunny had been paying Ada privately all along, of course, but now Ada had a job she could proudly display on her resume, when she moved on. She'd have to do that, someday.

"College," Bunny insisted to Ada.

"Art school," Ada had said wistfully. "It's just not practical. If I had the money—But I don't. I have to be practical." She got a stubborn look on her face. "You didn't go to college, Miz Dowdy, and you're doing just fine."

When Gina was down for the weekend, she helped Ada think it through, better than Bunny could. "What about community college certificates in graphic design?" she suggested.

Bunny, listening in, was starting to get an idea. She was starting to make some inquiries.

Meanwhile, there was a lot of work to running a nonprofit.

"Don't forget about yourself, Bunny," Charlie told her.

"You know, I'm pretty well fixed. I don't need a salary."

"It will look better to charitable grant makers if you do give yourself a salary, though," he argued. "Doesn't have to be much. Makes your organization look legit, not a rich woman's hobby."

"Okay," said Bunny. They were cozied up before a fire in Charlie's huge rec room.

"Bunny—" Charlie was giving her a strange look.

"What? This is so romantic, Charlie! Looks like it might even snow. Christmas is coming. A Southern white Christmas. Is anything better? Hot buttered rum, mmm."

Charlie interrupted Bunny's nervous burbling. "Look, Bunny. I've been doing some thinking."

The Patented Bunny Radar had begun pinging big-time at the start of this conversation of theirs, and Bunny wasn't sure she liked the direction she thought it might take.

She was right. Charlie pulled out a little velvet box and flipped it open. Inside nestled a ring with the most freakishly large diamond solitaire Bunny had ever set eyes on. "Marry me, Bunny."

"Umm." Bunny laughed a little. "Is that the Hope Diamond?"

"It's my hope, Bunny. My hope you'll say yes."

"But Charlie, I don't—"

He put the ring box down carefully on the big slab of a coffee table and took her hands in his. "Bunny. You and I are grown-ups, not starry-eyed kids. You're about to say you don't love me. Aren't you."

Bunny blushed and looked down.

"I know we've talked about. . ." he hesitated. "People we've known. Disappointments. I understand all that." He pressed her hands gently. "That doesn't matter, Bunny. What matters is that we like each other. We're friends. We have respect, companionship. I've done the whole love thing, as you know. It did not go well, left a bad taste in my mouth. And I know, from things you've said, that you probably feel the same. You're not a naïve girl any longer. You haven't been married, but you've been in a lot of relationships, including a serious one that left you pretty destroyed. Is it too soon? Is that it? Hey, we're good friends, you and I. We're good in bed together, aren't we?" He gave her a roguish smile.

Her heart kind of melted. "Yes, we are," she said, dimpling up. A little voice deep inside insisted, *yes, but Finn*. She told the little voice to shut up. No point in thinking about Finn. None at all. That was a different time. A different man. Its own unique thing, and now that unique thing was a closed chapter in her life.

"We'll travel." Charlie looked so eager. She shrank from hurting him. "Now that your rescue is on a solid footing, you can leave day-to-day operations to Ada when we do. I've reached a point in my career where I can get away for stuff like that. Let me show you the world, Bunny."

She hesitated. "All that sounds wonderful, Charlie. I do like and respect you. You're a wonderful friend and companion. I need some time to think about this, though."

"Take all the time you need, Bunny. Anything to make you comfortable and happy. I want to take care of you."

"You're a lot more sophisticated than I am, Charlie. Art, culture. All that."

"Who cares about that when you have friendship and respect?" he said. "All that other stuff you can learn. Being a good person deep down—not sure you can learn that. And you are, Bunny. A good person." His eyes went dreamy. "Do you know, when we were in high school together, I used to watch you. The nerd kid, pressing his nose against the glass as the popular kids had fun doing all the stuff I was too shy to do—dating, going to prom, being cheerleaders. That cheerleader skirt looked great on you, Bunny. And the tight sweater!" Charlie mock-shivered.

Bunny had to giggle. The whole cheerleader thing. Something out of another life. She was good enough to be head cheerleader. She could leap and do splits, and she had a loud voice. And loud hair. Not good enough for prom queen, though. That role always went to one of the rich girls. "High school." She made a little face.

"Back then I used to wonder what it would be like to be you, Bunny. To be with you."

Bunny laughed out loud at that. "Just silly small-town high school stuff. Big frogs in small ponds." She thought about fullback Bo, the Big Dog, the biggest dog in the smallest pound. Go, Crabbers. "And all that time, you were the smart kid who made it out and for real made it big."

Ignoring that, he leaned in for a kiss. "You were so pretty, Bunny. You still are." Bunny, feeling his reassuring lips on hers, began to argue to herself that he must be right about what they had together. She did feel taken care of, around Charlie.

"You had a hard life, too," he said, pulling back. "I really admired you back then. The sad thing that happened to your mother. Having to live with your great-aunt. But you were so plucky. You grabbed your life and didn't let go. You never do let go, do you? Look at your career, and what you did to revive it. And now look at what you're accomplishing in animal rescue. You're pretty, but I admire you, too. You're no frilly little trinket. I worry that men might treat you as if you are. I never will. I'll never make that mistake. You're real, Bunny. If I had to describe you, that's the word I'd use. Real. Say yes."

When she left Raleigh early to get back to Currituck Cove in time for the Monday morning parrot tour, Bunny still felt torn. She promised Charlie an answer soon. But she couldn't answer yet.

Everything Charlie said made sense.

He'd let her have her own life. He'd never interfere with that.

And they'd go off traveling, see art and go to plays, and— the prospect of the life they'd lead was dazzling. As dazzling as the diamond, which she had left with Charlie.

Bunny loved pretty things. The diamond was magnificent. But she realized something about herself. She loved other things more.

Back in Currituck Cove, she scrubbed the makeup off her face. She showered and put on jeans, a tee, a windbreaker against the winter chill. She pulled her hair back into a messy ponytail and headed for the aviary.

"How did the weekend go?" she greeted Ada.

"Great, Miz Dowdy. We had a nice sign-up for the tour, considering it's winter. Some folks are down here for a cozy beach Christmas, I guess. One family said this was their second time through the parrot tour."

"We're getting to be an institution," said Bunny. "Just wait'll beach season!" Bunny realized she'd have to hire at least one more staff member for beach season. She made plans to hire and train that person now, so she'd be all set when the shelter needed the extra hands.

Ada let them into the aviary and led Bunny from parrot to parrot, pointing out behavior quirks and feeding problems. Through it all, Saz perched on Bunny's shoulder, giving her love nips and parrot kisses, making a kind of purring sound. "Bunnneeee. Bunnneeee," he told her.

Just beyond the mesh of the shelter, Bingo waited patiently. He knew he was not allowed to go in, but he knew he was a good dog, too, and that Bunny would come out soon to take him for a walk up the winter beach. He frisked around a little. He knew all the signs. Bunny had his leash draped over her arm!

After Bingo's walk, Bunny and Ada went into the house where Bunny had refitted her pantry for quarantine duty.

"I'm worried this one is sick," said Ada.

They stood back examining the beautiful sun conure carefully. The petite bird's plumage looked dull. It sat listlessly on its perch, its food uneaten.

"Trip to Dr. Bekele in this one's future," said Bunny. "The near future. Back to Raleigh tomorrow. Quick turnaround." She laughed. But that was a good thing. Charlie deserved an answer to his question, and when she answered, she wanted it to be face to face.

The answer, though. She wasn't sure. Yes. Or no.

One thing she was sure about. Some creatures needed rescuing. The bird in front of them was one.

But do I need rescuing? she thought. *I want to take care of you*, Charlie had told her.

Did someone need to take care of her? No one ever had before. *Care for. Take care of.*

And

Care about.

She was still thinking about the difference as she and Ada went back out to the shelter to start the day's tour. Already a line had formed.

By this time, Bunny didn't need any notes, but she grabbed up a sheaf of brochures that Gina had designed for her. Bunny had insisted on paying the printing costs, even though Gina insisted just as stubbornly on donating her design expertise. "We're a real non-profit," Bunny had told Gina proudly.

"Yeah, and this is how I'm donating to it," Gina had said.

Thinking these thoughts, Bunny hadn't checked out the people in line yet. Usually she did.

She needed to check the visitors over. Any older people in the group who might have mobility issues, like Aunt Fanny? She had a bench for that. Sondra Martin had found the perfect one and had set it up for Bunny.

Any kids who might get rowdy and scare the birds without meaning to? Ada was ready to steer them off into a separate playground area with a bouncy parrot on springs. Joe Chasin the hardware store man and his sons had made that thing for Bunny.

Just as the tour was about to start, Bunny remembered she needed to look over the people in line.

She raised her gaze to a pair of incredibly green eyes.

Not parrot green. But really, really green.

In a panic, she turned to Ada. "Do me a solid and take over the tour? I'm not feeling well. Something I ate." She made a bolt for the house as Ada said behind her, "Hey, that man, second in line? Isn't he the guy who used to—"

Since you've been gone

BUNNY SAT FROZEN PANIC-stricken on the sofa in her living room, the once lovely piece of furniture that had now, to put it kindly, seen better days.

Finn, went the little voice in her head. *Finn. Finn.*

She couldn't meet Saz's eye. Saz got agitated during the tours sometimes, so mostly Bunny kept him in his cage.

Saz was agitated now.

Could he possibly understand?

Of course not. He was an animal. He didn't.

Bunny wrung her hands. What did it mean, Finn outside her house, lined up for the tour? She couldn't think, couldn't think at all.

She was just a big ball of feelings, and the big ball was settling in a leaden weight right down on top of her stomach. She thought she might throw up.

She grabbed a coffee from the Keurig machine and sipped it from one of their new shipments of Sazarac's Place mugs, for sale at the little stand Ada and Bunny decided they would one day turn into a gift shop.

Coffee, the cure for all ills. It wasn't working now. The coffee didn't settle her down. Bunny sighed at herself. Of course the coffee had exactly the opposite effect on her nerves. She sat hunched over with it on her formerly nice sofa. At least the warmth of the mug was comforting as her shaking hands wrapped around it.

When she heard the front door open, she leaped to her feet.

Thank god. Ada. "Is he gone?" she said.

"Miz Dowdy, uh, he said he wanted to see Saz."

Right behind her came Finn.

Ada turned a bright scarlet and darted back out of the house.

With an effort, Bunny tried to control her voice. Failed. The name came out in a croak. "Finn."

Behind her, Saz screamed out, a scream of joy. "Therrrre's Finn!"

Finn stepped to the cage. "Saz," he said softly. He half-turned to Bunny. "Mind if I take him out?"

"Sure, go ahead." She looked around wildly for some escape. There was none. Finn was here, the walking, talking green-eyed embodiment of her shame and hurt, and there was nothing she could do about it.

Finn opened the cage door and eased his hand in. Saz stepped up. Finn brought him out, and he zipped to Finn's shoulder and sat preening him and purring.

Somehow Bunny regained her normal voice. Sort of. Somehow she got to her feet. She and Finn faced off with the coffee table between them. "Saz is happy to see you."

"And you're not." Finn gave her a level look.

Bunny didn't reply.

Finn laughed a little, but the laugh didn't reach his eyes. "*Is he gone?* That's what you said to Ada, just now. Guess I shouldn't have come."

"I'm glad you're here." Bunny swallowed hard, balling her hands into fists and shoving them into her jeans pockets. "It was just a shock. You could have called."

"I was worried you'd tell me not to come."

"You're the one who blocked me," Bunny pointed out.

"And you, I believe, are the one who dumped me." The green eyes flashed anger. "You're the dumper. I'm the dumpee." His finger stabbed at her chest across the coffee table barrier.

They stood too far apart for any contact, but just the same, she jerked back, and he looked embarrassed. Before the tension between them could escalate, Bingo bounded into the room, frolicking around Finn until he knelt down so Bingo could give him many dog kisses.

Thank you, Bingo, Bunny said inside. "Here." She pointed to the sofa. "Sit down while I get us something to drink."

"I don't need anything—"

She pointed at the sofa. "Please. I need to collect my wits."

He sat.

She came back from the kitchen with a glass of iced tea for Finn, unsweetened. He was a Yankee, after all. And a Diet Cheerwine for her.

"Still glowing in the dark, I see," said Finn, taking the glass from her.

They sat in silence for a few moments. "What brings you down here from Raleigh?" she said at last.

"Raleigh." He looked blank. "What do you mean."

"Aren't you—I mean, don't you live in Raleigh?" She felt she was beginning to get a headache. Maybe he'd leave soon. Then she could untangle the ball of feelings in her gut. But while he was sitting right there beside her, it just wound tighter.

He stared at her, clearly mystified. "No, I don't live in Raleigh. I live in Manhattan, Kansas. Or, well, until last week Kansas. Now, I don't know."

"I thought—well, I thought you had taken that job in Raleigh."

"What job? Bunny, I don't know what's going on here, but why don't we dial it back a little. Let's just catch up a little on our lives. We're old friends, aren't we?"

"Are we?"

A look of pain crossed his face. "Do you want me to leave?"

"No," she said, realizing she meant it. The ball of feelings was beginning to settle down and sort itself out. "I'm glad you're here," she said again, knowing more this time that she meant it. "Saz and Bingo are glad you're here. Saz, stop that."

Saz was busy picking a loop of yarn out of Finn's big saggy sweater and beginning to unravel it.

Finn reached up a hand and absently scratched Saz on the back of the head, in the place he loved to be scratched.

"So let's catch up," said Finn. "You first. What's all this? This is remarkable, Bunny, what you've done here."

She felt herself smiling. "Yeah. It's great."

"What happened to the lipstick? What happened to the Lipstick Goddess?"

"Sold her. Sold her to that big company. You remember."

"Yeah, I do. And I remember thinking, Bunny is gonna regret this. But then I thought, Maybe, but Bunny will just start a new cosmetics company, and it will be bigger than ever."

"Instead, I started something completely different."

"Wow. Yes, you did."

"I got a lot of money for selling the idea and the name and the products to that big company, and with the money, I started this." Bunny waved her arms around. "All this. But Finn. Some of that money is due to you. The success of those products, that was due to you. I tried getting in touch with you. I swear I did. My lawyer told me I shouldn't keep trying, that I had no obligation to you. But I do, Finn."

"No, you don't. I won't take a penny from you, Bunny. I don't need the money, for one. And look what you've done with it, for two."

"But giving you a fair share is the right thing to do." She was beginning to shiver. "But I wanted to do it." She gulped. "But you blocked me, Finn." For the first time, tears started into her eyes.

Finn put his glass of iced tea carefully down on Bunny's scarred and bird-pooped-on formerly lovely coffee table. He looked as though he were about to take her in his arms, but he didn't. He moved toward her a little and put his hands on the knees of his khakis as if he wanted to chain them down there so they wouldn't fly up and grab her their ownselves.

He leaned toward her. "Bunny, what happened that day? What the fuck happened? I thought, no, not Bunny. Then I thought, Finn, you goof, she got what she wanted. I thought. . ." His voice trailed off. In a whisper he said, almost as if he were talking to himself, "She used me, she got what she wanted, then she dumped me. Not like it hadn't happened before, getting dumped. Told my-self what a fool I was, letting it happen to me twice. But now." He looked up and fixed his eyes on hers. "Now I'm not sure I do know what happened between the two of us. Can you help me under-stand that, Bunny? If you can, I'll be a grateful man. Because ever since you left me sitting on the side of the bed with nothing but a towel and a hard-on, I've been eating my liver over it."

Bunny shivered harder, replaying that scene in her mind.

A determined look settled in those green eyes of his. "I've thought about it. Thought over and over. What happened to change things didn't happen the day you left. It didn't happen that morning. It happened the day before. We were fine. Then we weren't. But what?" Now he looked directly at her. "Tell me what happened, Bunny."

Bunny didn't answer. "Finn. You tell me something. Are you working for Rona Petreius?" she said instead.

"What? No. What gave you that—oh." He stared at her, puzzled. "I met with her in Atlanta, that time. She wanted me to work for some company she was starting. She gave me a bunch of paperwork to look over." He shrugged. "I threw it away. I hear that company is a big deal now. Whatever. I didn't want anything to do with it. And not with her, not ever again."

Bunny found herself shaking her head. "Oh, man," she whispered.

"What?"

"I thought—"

"Did you know about her offer, somehow? Is that why you left? How could you know that?"

Bunny opened her mouth to spin some story about how she'd heard about it as she strolled through the conference. Some lie or other that wouldn't make her look like an eavesdropper and a sneak. She closed her mouth again and shook her head.

"Bunny."

"I was wrong, Finn. What I did was wrong." Now the tears did start to leak down her cheeks. She brushed them angrily away. "I eavesdropped on you and Rona. At lunch."

"But how—" he began. Then he shook his head. "Doesn't matter how. So you overheard her make this offer, and you believed I would take it? You believed I took it? How could you think that? And why wouldn't you just ask?" From bewildered, he was starting to look angry again. "Dammit, Bunny."

"You have every right to be angry, Finn. I did think those things. And I thought, see, this woman, she's right for you. And I'm—" Bunny gulped. "I'm wrong for you. And I thought—" Now the words were coming out in a rush. She couldn't have stopped them if she'd wanted to. She didn't want to stop them.

No. Her mouth gaped open in a panic. She did want to stop them.

Finn reached for her and took her hands in his. "Just say it, Bunny," he whispered. "Say it all."

Bunny wasn't paying attention. She was thinking about Like a Boss Red Rona. "And see, I thought she's so smart, and so are you, and you're too young for me, and I'm too dumb for you, and she's so beautiful and elegant in that way of hers—" She laughed a little. That's when she realized he was holding onto her hands. She didn't pull them away. "See what a mess I am, Finn. I'm so much older than you. My house is a wreck, I'm a wreck." She was suddenly aware of her lack of make-up, a few too many laugh-lines around her eyes, her messy hair, nails chipped. Even her jeans had a rip in them. She took in a breath. She made herself go on. "And I thought, this woman Rona, she's still in love with you, and she's offering you this job to make it right, and it's the job you deserve, and you're still in love with her, and all the pain will go away." She wound down at last. "That's what I thought," she said in a small voice.

Finn's eyes narrowed. "You sit here and tell me you think I was still in love with that woman?"

"I heard the pain in your voice, Finn. I heard it." Bunny was remembering the whole scene now, as if it were unrolling like a movie in her head. "You were in pain."

"Damn right I was in pain. That woman betrayed me. She played me, Bunny. And I let her. I kind of hated myself, until I met you, and realized there was some goodness in the world. I thought there was." He said the last thing in a whisper. He let go her hands.

"Oh, Finn!" she cried, overwhelmed.

Both animals rushed to her, Bingo to lean against her knee, Saz to preen her.

"And another thing," he said gruffly, setting his mouth in a thin angry line. "You're not a wreck. Look at you, Bunny. You are a gorgeous woman. And dumb? You're anything but dumb. Look what you've started. Right in your own back yard, too. Give you a long-enough lever and you could move the world. Whoever let you think otherwise, I'd like to give them a punch in the jaw."

His hands stole back toward hers, and she found herself grabbing them and holding on to them the way a drowning person holds on to the lifeguard.

Then they were in each other's arms.

What the animals thought about that, they never did remember.

Just that Ada stepped into the room, yelped, and backed out again. "What's wrong with me today? My timing is for shit," they heard her mutter as she closed the door.

All up in everyone's business

IT HAD TO BE DONE. Bunny would not let herself put it off, as much as she dreaded the moment. The moment she'd have to say no to Charlie Pounder

Three days with Finn, and her head was spinning. But that didn't mean their problems had gone away. She and Finn, they might not end up together. They might not, Bunny insisted to herself. She poured a cup of coffee into her black *Life's a Bitch, Then You Die* mug and was sipping it at the little table in her kitchen, Saz on her shoulder trying his damnedest to pick her favorite jeweled barrette out of her hair, Bingo curled up over the tops of her feet.

"Ow, Saz."

Bunny's lips curved into a smile. "What do you mean, might not end up together?" That's what Finn had said, outraged, as he left to drive down the coast the day before. "We ARE ending up together, Bunny Dowdy."

"But we might not," she argued. "We're too different."

"That again." He had rolled his eyes. "Okay, I have to do a site visit. The National Fish and Wildlife Service works with an endangered marsh down in Hyde County," he explained briefly. "Then I'm coming back through, and we're having this out between us. It's gonna be over, Bunny. Over."

"You mean we're gonna be over? Is that what you mean?" She found she couldn't resist teasing him. She had missed that so much.

"Don't twist my words, woman." He had leaned out the window to give her a kiss that left her breathless. Then he had backed out of her driveway in his rental car and had headed south.

Now, at her little kitchen table, all the riled-up emotions inside her gone quiet at last, she could think things through.

She needed to go to Raleigh and say no to Charlie.

It didn't matter whether she and Finn did or didn't work out. It didn't matter at all. The decision would have to be the same. And now she realized. That decision was always going to be the same.

It was no.

It was always going to be no.

As much as she liked and valued Charlie, Bunny didn't love him.

Because Bunny knew she did love a man.

And she knew that man was Finn.

And that made all the difference.

If one of the many, many things between her and Finn kept them apart in the end, it still didn't matter. And they might, she argued with the absent Finn. Keep us apart, she insisted to him. So many things.

Whatever. Whichever.

It made absolutely no difference to the decision about Charlie.

She wasn't settling. And she didn't think Charlie should settle, either.

Life was too precious to settle. Love was too precious.

When Charlie opened his door to her several hours later, he turned aside with a wry smile. "You've made a decision," he told her. "And it's no."

"I'm sorry, Charlie." She grabbed him in a hug, and he hugged her back.

"Your answer's all over you, Bunny. Well, I tried, give me that much."

"Oh, Charlie," she said, sinking down into his luxurious leather couch. "If only I could say yes. I like you so much."

"It's that other guy, isn't it?" he said, bringing her a beautiful light and crisp white wine. "Finn."

She stared at him, startled.

"Sheesh, Bunny. Ever since we reconnected, it's been Finn this and Finn that. And then, the hurt in your eyes. Think I don't know what that's like? A memory, such a sweet one, and the second it pops into your mind, the hurt chases in right after it. But whoever this Finn guy was, he was gone. I thought—" He looked down into his glass. "I thought maybe I had a chance."

"Didn't realize I talked about him all the time like that. Gaah. Charlie, you should have run the other way, when we met up again. You know what they say about rebounds. Too much baggage." She took a sip of wine. Then she looked him in the eye. "I really thought about what you said. About companionship, and seeing the world together, and everything. I really did, Charlie. I could see we'd have a lovely life together. Don't think I want to throw that away. I just, when I thought it through, just knew it would never work out."

"Did you know you murmured his name one time, when we were in bed?"

"Lordy. Charlie, why didn't you throw me out. I'm so embarrassed. I'm such a mess."

"Don't be embarrassed." Charlie grinned at her.

"At least no hearts are getting broken here," said Bunny, grinning back. "Don't get me wrong. Friendship is a great basis for a marriage. I'm guessing people marry for friendship all the time, and I'm guessing most of them make it work. Make it work just fine."

But she flinched at what she saw in his eyes. He was lying when he'd said he just thought of her as a friend. Hearts WERE getting broken here. And that hurt. Lord, did it hurt. Good friends were like gold, and hurting one? Not what she wanted. Couldn't be helped.

"Friends. Yes. We could have been good together." He and Bunny both pretended there was no false note in his voice when he said it.

"I hope we can stay friends," said Bunny.

"Always," said Charlie. "Besides, I'm your lawyer."

"You can't be making anything on my tiny nonprofit!"

"We lawyers call that kind of thing pro bono work. Looks good when we start polishing our medals."

They sat silently drinking their wine.

"Look," he said after a moment. "He's back, right? Finn? I think I must be right about that."

"Yes. But Charlie." She put her hand on his arm. "I've thought about that a lot. Suppose he hadn't come back. Would I have agreed to marry you if he hadn't? The answer would still have been no. I mean, it still might not work out between me and Finn. But I can't marry you, no matter what happens with that. . . that other thing."

"I understand," he said.

She thought he did, too. Because once you know about love. . .she shivered. Once you know love, all bets are off.

He made her dinner, delicious as always. She cut off the wine so she'd be good to drive back, after, and he gave her a wistful kiss as she left.

The next week passed in a blur. She and Ada worked furiously to get ready for the Christmas season. It was coming right at them. There were sure to be Christmas beach visitors to Currituck Cove, especially now that the new golf club was such a draw, and that meant Christmas parrot tours.

Bunny and Ada kicked around various ideas. Santa hats for the parrots.

Nope. A hard no. They tried a test hat out on Saz. They found it demolished by the end of the day. Saz stalked back and forth disdainfully over the tattered remains.

They settled for red bows festooning the aviary, and special Christmas-themed parrot toys they wouldn't put out until the last minute.

Joe Chapin did have the inspired idea to put a little Santa hat on the bouncy-parrot, though, and Gina sent them special Santa-hatted parrot logos and banners and Christmas tour brochures, so it all worked out.

The aviary had become so much a part of the town by then—"That fast!" Ada marveled—that Sazarac's Place wangled a last-minute spot on the Currituck Cove annual Christmas house tour when one of the rich homeowners backed out. "Our tour's gonna be such a hit they'll invite us back for next year before they ask anyone else," Bunny declared. On her shoulder, Saz chimed in with a "Good birrrrrrd."

"Next year, a parrot-themed float for the Christmas parade," Bunny and Ada promised each other. They'd recruit high school aviary volunteers, and the high schoolers could decorate the float.

Always, in the back of her mind, Bunny thought about what would happen when Finn returned from his site visit. In their few days together, he'd told her what he had been doing when they left each other over a year earlier.

The job he'd mentioned as a maybe in Atlanta hadn't been with Rona Petreius at all. It was a job as a government contractor, short-term but very well paying. He'd taken it. "I told myself, just a stopgap, and good for the c.v."

At her look of confusion, he amended, "Resume. But then they re-upped my one-year contract for at least one more year." The government work had moved him three times in the space of a year and a half: to Washington, D.C., to New Mexico, and most recently to Kansas.

Now he was headed for a quick assignment to assess the ground water of a marsh pretty far down the coast from Currituck Cove. "Agricultural runoff," he explained. "Always a threat, and that last hurricane made it worse. Lots of possible damage from fertilizers and pesticides."

Hurricane Janelle. Bunny had nodded sagely, as if she understood half of what he was telling her. She got the gist, though. There was a threat to the animals and other creatures of the marsh, and Finn was on it.

His assignment would only take a few weeks. So he had checked in to a bad motel somewhere near Swanquarter and was spending the week with U.S. Fish and Wildlife Service biologists there, who would figure out how Finn could shoulder some of the testing load to assess the damage. Or something. "Those guys hate contractors, though. Probably not gonna be a pleasant week," he said as he left. "Besides, you know where my mind will be."

They exchanged a smile so full of promise that Bunny felt a fluttering and a tingling she hadn't enjoyed since Atlanta.

She might as well have installed one of those digital countdown gizmos in her brain. *Three more days til Finn is back. . . Two more days. . . One more day. . .*

The day of Finn's return was one of the great sunny winter days the beach enjoys sometimes, and it promised well for the Christmas tours. The weather report said the good weather would hold for the coming week.

So Bunny was feeling positively exuberant, if kinda frustrated and hot and bothered. She knew Finn wasn't due back for hours. She was trying not to think about it. Failing.

At least there was a lot to keep her busy. To keep her mind off Finn. Sort of.

Ada and Bunny ushered the last of the day's tour visitors to the little visitor stand/gift kiosk they had set up at the path leading from the backyard curving around to Beachcomber Road. They had just totted up the last of the many mugs they had sold that day. Ada bent over the screen of her ipad's point of sale app, where she had cleverly inserted a check-box: *Make a tax-deductible donation to Sazarac's Place!*

"We gotta get teeshirts for beach season," Bunny was just saying, when something caught at the corner of her eye.

Bunny turned.

A woman stood there.

"Sorry, ma'am, we just finished today's tour, but come back tomorrow," Ada called out.

Bunny put a hand on her arm. "No. This is someone to see me, Ada. Go ahead and go home early. I have something to talk over with this woman."

Ada caught a glimpse of Bunny's expression and hurried for the house.

The woman stepped forward. Expensively put together. Elegant. Lovely oval face.

With lipstick too pale for her, Bunny thought automatically.

"Ms. Dowdy," said the woman. Her tone was polite and even.

"Yes."

"I'm Rona Petreius." She held out a hand.

Bunny ran her own hands down her jeans. "Dirty hands," she murmured. She was suddenly aware of the calluses on her hands, and how frumpy she looked, compared to this woman. Bunny was in jeans and a flannel shirt. *And a stupid Santa hat*, she thought in despair, jerking it off and laying it aside.

"Look. I'll get straight to the point," said Rona. "Don't hire Finn Johansen."

But I'm not hiring. . . Bunny started to say. Different words entirely marched out of her mouth. "I'll hire whomever I please, Ms. Petreius."

"Dr. Petreius," said Rona.

"I see," said Bunny.

"This place." Rona's eyes flicked around dismissively. "Some amateur backyard animal shelter. Finn is a professional. You'd be exploiting him."

Bunny heard a cough. She turned toward the sound, and so did Rona Petreius.

Finn lounged against one of the aviary's posts. "So gratifying to hear you're looking out for my welfare, Rona," he said.

Rona Petreius didn't miss a beat. "Finn. Come to your senses. Government work? That's beneath you. But this! You're kidding me, right?"

Bunny opened her mouth to say something. She closed it.

Finn didn't say anything, either.

Two bright spots flared across Rona's beautiful cheekbones. "Finn. Come work for me. It's what you've always wanted."

"You keep telling me that, Rona. But we both know your company has no intention of actually doing any meaningful work on animal welfare." He raised a hand to forestall her objection. "Not that it matters what your company intends. What you intend. I'll never work for you. Or with you. Get out of here, Rona. Get out of my business. Get out of my life. I've asked you nicely, and now I'm telling you."

"What?" she threw a scornful glance at Bunny. "For her? For this?"

"I'll work for whoever I want to work for," said Finn. "I'll be with whoever I want to be with."

"You're a fool," said Rona.

Bunny was busy on her phone. "Officer Gould?" she said into it. "Yeah. Bunny. Hey, Bill, think you could come over here? There's a trespasser who won't leave. Yeah. Thanks." She clicked off. The look she gave Rona could strip paint. "Finn's not a fool, no matter who he decides to work for or what he wants to do with his life, and we both know it. You, however, ma'am." Bunny felt herself getting all flustered up. "Well, bless your black little shrunk-up heart. You are a manipulator and a poser, and you can kiss my go-to-hell."

Rona gasped. "You see how common and vulgar this woman is," she huffed to Finn. "How could you lower yourself?"

Finn was heading toward her with a glint in his eye when they all heard the siren.

Rona turned on her heel and started to leave.

"Wait," said Bunny.

"What?" she bit out.

"Scarlet."

"What?" Her look moved from furious to confused.

"Lipstick," said Bunny, as patiently as she could. "You need a very bright brilliant red on those pale lips of yours."

Rona began backing white-faced out of the yard.

"Free advice. My gift to you," Bunny called after her. She almost chased Rona down, to give her a sample of Like a Boss Red. Nahhh. Maybe not.

She and Finn stood listening, hardly breathing. The sound of a car motor starting up came to them from around the house. A very expensive sound.

"Her beemer," said Finn. They listened as it accelerated up Beachcomber Road.

When Officer Gould and Ada burst into the back yard, Bunny and Finn were having some kind of stare-down.

Bunny stopped staring to explain the situation to both of them.

"You want me to cite her?" said Officer Gould, looking eager. "I think that's the speeder I passed, coming in. I could get her on that, too."

"Nah," said Bunny. "I don't think she'll be back. But I thank you kindly, Bill. Your siren scared her off."

"You scared her off, Bunny," muttered Finn. "The crazy parrot lady."

When they were alone, Bunny trusted herself to look at Finn again. He was shaking his head. Biting his lip.

"Don't you dare laugh at me, Finn Johansen."

"I wouldn't dream of it, Bunny Dowdy." He took her by the arm and led her toward the house.

As he steered her in the direction of the bedroom, he was murmuring, "You can take the Lipstick Goddess out of the back yard, but you can't take the back yard. . ."

"That doesn't even make sense, Finn," Bunny complained. "Why am I forever and always up in other folks' business?" she said to no one in particular.

"How about I get up in your business," he whispered in her ear. "How about right now, right here?"

He was already stealing his hands up the back of her flannel shirt to undo the clasp of her bra, and she was already reaching behind her for the zipper to his khakis.

Down south by the border

"THERE'S SOMETHING I don't quite get," said Bunny, as the morning sun streamed in on them.

"Hold that thought and wait right there," said Finn. "I'm gonna bring coffee up here to you."

He came back with coffee in a Sazarac's Place mug for him, and one of her new favorites, *Love Hurts* stenciled over a picture of a parrot nipping a finger.

They lay sipping the fragrant coffee together, but he kept one hand on her. "I'm not taking my hands off you, Bunny." His voice had gone kind of raspy, if you asked Bunny.

With her own free hand, she felt around. "Oh, man," she said.

They both carefully set their mugs down and by the time they picked them up again, the coffee was cold.

"Good thing it's a Sunday," said Bunny. "No parrot tour." Then she realized she had never gotten an answer to her question. "Umm, Finn?"

"What?" he turned a sleepy eye on her, and that delicious curve of the lips.

"When you and Rona had that taxicab standoff in the backyard?"

"A what?"

"A taxicab standoff."

"I think you mean—uh. That's a very racist thing to say, Bunny."

"Taxicabs are racist?" She blinked.

"Never mind. What were you going to say about the, uh, stand-off?"

"Well, Rona pretty obviously marched into my back yard to save you from yourself."

He grunted.

"I mean, she thought you were about to go to work for me. At Sazarac's Place."

"Yeah. I guess."

"Why did she think that, Finn? I mean, I have been wondering ever since she said her piece back there. Well, not ever since, because a lot of the time I haven't been thinking of her at all, I've been thinking about—"

"What, about this?"

"Ah. Yes. About that. And. . .what was I saying?"

"I don't know." He gave her a kiss and deepened it. "What were you saying?"

She didn't answer. She was too busy. They were too busy.

But later, when they finally did haul themselves out of bed, she made him look at her. "I want a straight answer, Finn. What the frick did Rona Petreius mean when she came into my back yard to try to convince you not to go to work for me? Why would she think that? I mean, you're a scientist with a well-paying government job. Why would you ever do a thing like that? Like you were desperate or something. I mean, what the fork?"

"Bunny."

"Don't Bunny me. Answer the question."

"Uh. She may have thought I was considering it."

"Considering going to work at Sazarac's Place?"

"Yeah. Wanna get pizza at Mervin and Bob's for lunch?"

She reached up to grab him by the shoulders. A bit hard, because he was a lot taller than she was. She tugged him down so they saw eye to eye. "Why would she have thought anything of the kind?"

"Because I may have said I was thinking about it?"

"Finn."

"Bunny."

"You can't."

"Why not?"

"All the reasons we just said. All the reasons Rona just trotted out of her too-pale bitch lips. You're too smart. You're a professional. You don't need another shit job, certainly not some amateur thing in someone's back yard. I believe that's how Rona the Bitch Goddess put it, and she was right. Don't you have your new assignment coming up soon?"

"In Dayton, Ohio. Yep."

"And?"

"What's to say I can't do both?"

"You can't be in Dayton, Ohio, and Currituck Cove, North Carolina at the same time. That's why."

"Why not? Umm, see, there's this cat, and maybe it's in the box and maybe it's not, because. . ."

"Finn!"

"Look, Bunny. So, I just had to do a site visit, right? I drove down the coast, and I spent a week there covered in Deet. And by the way. Don't use Deet. It's bad for birds."

"Finn—"

"But then I'll go back to my apartment in Kansas and crunch numbers and do internet research. And that's mostly what I do. Crunch numbers, cruise the 'net, then write up the findings."

"I thought you liked more hands-on stuff, like being in a lab, and stuff."

"I do."

"So why—"

"It pays the bills. It's a good job. If I play it right, I'll move from contractor to working directly for the Feds, and I've been given to understand that's definitely in the cards. The pay won't be quite as good, but the benefits and job security will be better. Or I could just keep doing contract work. Might suit me better, especially since I don't have a family, don't have to think too hard about benefits like good insurance and that. But you're right. There's a loss. Something I've struggled with. I do like the hands-on stuff. And another thing. Suppose the no family situation changes?"

"So you're saying—"

"So I'm saying I might live in Kansas right now—not for long, I might add—but I don't have to stay in Kansas to do my job. If I'm shifted to Dayton, Ohio, or Kalamzaoo—"

"Or Shangri-la."

"The ignorance of you Southerners about the Midwest. There really is a Kalamazoo." At her skeptical look, he added, "It's in Michigan. It's a great little college town with a fantastic Greek restaurant."

"You're changing the subject again," she said.

"I could live anywhere and do my job, as long as I have an internet connection and a close-by airport. I could live here and do my job."

Her breath caught in her throat.

"And during the times I'm here, I could help out with Sazarac's Place. So I could get my hands-on fix. But you know what?"

"What?"

"I could get my hands-on fix this way, too."

All thoughts of maybe getting lunch faded into the background.

They found themselves in Bunny's bed again.

Afterward, she sat up indignantly, pulling the sheets to her breasts.

When he tried yanking the sheets down again, she smacked his hand away. "You just want me for sex," she accused.

"You say that like it's a bad thing. Yes, I want you for sex. And. . ." He leaned over the side of the bed, feeling for his khakis. He pulled a little object out of his pants pocket and sat up, too. "And for this."

Gently he took one of her hands, the left, and guided the little object onto her ring finger.

It was a plastic parrot ring.

"Got it at that motel with the big tacky gift shop, you know the one, down across the South Carolina border?" he said, when she found she couldn't say a word.

Just stared down at her finger with the plastic parrot perched on it.

"Marry me, Bunny," he said huskily.

When she raised her eyes to his, they were glistening with tears.

He kissed them off as they slid one by one down her cheeks.

"Yes," she said.

Reverse harem

AS BUNNY AND FINN SPED west on highway 64 toward Raleigh, Bunny had at last brought herself to the ultimate act of trust. She was allowing Finn to drive the hotpinkmobile.

"She handles well," Finn admitted. He had given up his campaign to get Bunny to consider a more fuel-efficient, environmentally friendly ride. Sort of. He said nothing when she shelled out a small fortune to get the hotpinkmobile's alternator replaced. Then, as summer came on, the AC compressor. Well, almost nothing. He did mutter stuff like "Once they're past a certain age, they nickel and dime you to death." Oh, and "Buy a new AC compressor? Almost cheaper to buy a new car." But he didn't press it. Much.

The trip was enjoyable. "I'll be missing my guys, though," said Bunny.

"Ada will take good care of them both. You know that," said Finn.

"Yeah."

"Anyhow, what do you mean, *my guys*. Aren't I your guy?"

"One of them." Bunny dimpled up.

"Oh, I see. I get it now. You have the whole reverse-harem thing going on."

So the trip west passed pleasantly. At least until they got to the outskirts of Raleigh. Bunny's hand flew to her mouth and Finn compressed his mouth into a grim line. That ka-thunk, ka-thunk, ka-thunk. They both knew what that noise meant. They'd both owned clunkers in their day. They recognized that noise.

Luckily, a garage loomed up on the side of the road into Raleigh, and Finn steered the limping hotpinkmobile in.

Bunny and Finn spent an anxious hour fidgeting around the waiting room of the place drinking terrible coffee from the machine out of flimsy cardboard cups stamped *Honest Ron's*, not even printed. As if someone, maybe Ron, maybe he'd gotten his kids to do it, had bought a lot of bad cups and rubber stamped a bunch of them.

"Ma'am," said the mechanic. Ron himself, maybe. "Your car done thrown a rod."

"But how!" Bunny burst out. "I just had her serviced. I just had her oil changed." Her eyes narrowed. "You don't think somebody forgot to put the plug back in," she began.

"No, ma'am." The mechanic held up a grimy object. "After a long stretch, these plugs, they get brittle. They crack. They go."

"Oh," said Bunny. "How much to fix her."

"A heap more'n she's worth, and that's a fact."

"Oh, no," said Bunny.

By the next hour, Finn had made arrangements for the hotpinkmobile to be towed off to the junkyard. He had called the two of them an Uber. They had headed for the lot of an establishment that sold fuel-economical and environmentally friendly cars.

"Now, Bunny. I know you're in mourning. I know the thought of replacing the hotpinkmobile is more than you can handle just at the moment."

They were getting out of the Uber and a salesman was bustling over.

"So I'm going to buy us a car," Finn said, being firm about it.

As Bunny started to open her mouth to object, he cut her off. "I can afford it, Bunny. More than afford it. I insist. You can buy the next one."

They drove off the lot in a car boasting great fuel economy. It was so environmentally friendly that it had a little tree icon on the glowing high-tech panel that was apparently its dashboard.

"So we're all set. And later on, you can find another very pink automobile. Deal?"

Bunny looked disconsolately out of the passenger side window.

"This is a nice little vehicle, Bunny," Finn tried again. "What do you think of it? Now, be honest."

"It's beige," said Bunny.

"The sales guy called it champagne."

"That's marketing for you," Bunny said with a sigh.

"Well, it's a bubbly little car. Lotta pep. I like it." Finn gave her a bright smile which was not returned.

He made it up to her later at the nice hotel they sprung for, with the great king-sized bed.

In the morning, she was in a much better mood, and all ready for their visit to Aunt Fanny.

"I'm a little nervous. This is meet-the-family time," said Finn, tugging at his parrot tie.

"She is gonna love you."

"But I'm a Yankee," said Finn.

"Thought you said you weren't."

"Uh, technically no, but—"

"Shush, she'll love you. You're cute. You're polite. You're wearing a parrot tie, and she loves birds. She loves my birds."

"And you're wearing a parrot ring," he pointed out.

She glanced down at the plastic ring that had not left her finger from the moment Finn installed it there.

"So what's she gonna think of a man who proposed to her great-niece who is practically her daughter, and did it with a Crackerjacks prize?"

"I thought you said—"

"I'm speaking metaphorically."

"It'll be fine."

Bunny was right, it was. Although at first she had her doubts. She'd forgotten Aunt Fanny had seen right into her pain, and knew a man had done it to her. Bunny could tell Aunt Fanny saw this was the very man who had broken her Bunny's heart.

"You'll be good to my Bunny, won't you," she said to Finn. It was not a question. Her eyes bored into Finn's, becoming surprisingly sharp and astute.

"Yes, ma'am." It was as if Finn could read Aunt Fanny's mind. "We had a misunderstanding, and we were both pretty unhappy, but all it took was some common sense and some talking—"

And some fantastic sex, Bunny beamed at him.

"—and everything cleared right up," he concluded. "And Bunny is the woman for me. I love Bunny."

Hearing Finn say that made Bunny tear up.

Aunt Fanny beamed at him. Looked like she'd made up her mind about Finn, and now she could relax.

"Bunny, sweetie, I want to hear all about the birds. How is my Sazzie doing? And Bingo. Don't want to neglect Bingo."

They spent the next hour filling Aunt Fanny in on all the successes of Sazarac's Place, and all of the antics of Saz himself. And Bingo, of course.

"Well, you two are in for a treat. Remember I told you about my friend Edna's bird, Pirate Queen?"

"Aunt Fanny had a friend who owned a parrot," Bunny explained to Finn. "Sounds like it might have been a Senegal like Saz. Queenie," she said to Aunt Fanny. "I remember." To Finn she said, "It was very sad. Aunt Fanny's friend died."

"I got a call from the receptionist who said Edna's nephew is in town and wants to stop by and say a quick hello. Isn't that nice?" Aunt Fanny chirped.

Inwardly Bunny groaned. Meeting Edna's nephew didn't sound like the best way to spend the end of their Raleigh visit. But when she looked into Aunt Fanny's beaming face and fond old eyes, she sucked it up and said yes, it was very nice. Aunt Fanny had so few pleasures these days, and Edna had been her dearest friend.

The nephew was shown up to Aunt Fanny's sitting room. He shook Bunny's hand, and Finn's. Bunny could tell he sort of didn't know exactly who they were or why Aunt Fanny wanted him to meet them, but he was being as good a sport about it as they were.

He and Aunt Fanny reminisced about Edna.

"Yes, Edna was a lovely woman," the nephew told Bunny. "I was very fond of her. I was her only living relative. My wife and I had been out on the West Coast for years, though, so I hardly ever got to see her. Then my company sent me to the Netherlands, and that was only days after Edna died."

"Bad timing," Bunny murmured.

"At least we were here to see that all her wishes were honored, she got a nice funeral, all that."

"Very nice," said Aunt Fanny placidly.

"Anyway," the nephew went on, "the wife and I just got back to the States, and I had to come by and pay my respects to you, Miz

Fanny." He turned to Aunt Fanny. "You were such a good friend to Edna. You helped me so much with the arrangements, Miz Fanny. It was a helluva thing—begging your pardon, Miz Fanny—but we had to make all those arrangements for Edna, get in touch with the lawyers, do all sorts of odds and ends, when we were due to leave only a day or two after the funeral."

"I remember," said Aunt Fanny. "Now, this is such a nice coincidence. Remember Pirate Queen?"

"I surely do, Miz Fanny," said the nephew.

"Now, Bunny here has a parrot of a very similar type. She loves parrots."

"That is indeed interesting, Miz Fanny," said the nephew. Bunny thought his eyes had glazed over a bit.

Any second, he's going to make his excuses and get out of here, thought Bunny, *and then Finn and I can, too.*

"Now, what did happen to poor Queenie? She took on so after Edna passed. I was real worried about her," Aunt Fanny persisted. "Parrots sense these things, you know. They're very intelligent animals."

The nephew gave himself a little shake. "I hate to admit it," he said slowly. "but I don't know what happened to her. I feel terrible telling you that. Until you mentioned Queenie, I guess I had forgotten all about her. The wife and I had to pack up so fast, and—" He snapped his fingers. "I do remember now. My wife is a jewel. She's the one who took on the task of finding Queenie a new home. I'm not sure what she did find, though. Just she told me it was all taken care of."

Bunny's Patented Intuition was giving her an uncomfortable prod. She leaned forward. "Is your wife with you now? Could we ask her?"

The man looked over at Bunny, startled.

"I run a parrot rescue," Bunny explained. "I'm real interested in these things."

"Well, now. Suppose you don't approve of what we did." He gave her a little nervous laugh.

"Oh, don't be embarrassed. People never know what to do with a parrot when stuff happens, especially when the owner dies. That's especially difficult. I've seen it all, believe you me. I don't judge."

His smile looked a little weak. "I can find out for you. The wife's off shopping. I'll text her."

That's unfortunate, Finn signaled with his eyes. *We were just about to make our escape.*

Bunny stared down at her hands. Something was telling her she had to know.

The text came through pretty fast. It didn't leave Bunny in suspense long.

The nephew looked up brightly. "Oh, all's well with the parrot. I mean, I suppose it is. The wife found out that a friend of Edna's had a niece who might take the parrot, and she had the parrot shipped to the niece."

Bunny's tingling intensified.

"And," said the nephew, looking down at his phone, "the wife says she included a note saying if the niece couldn't keep Queenie, here was a list of places she could take her."

"So," said Finn drily. "Your wife kicked the can down the road, as it were."

Bunny shot him a warning look.

The nephew bridled a little. "We had to get on the plane to Europe the next day," he said. "We did the best we could."

"I'm sure you did," Bunny cut in soothingly. "Only, unfortunately, that note didn't make it with the parrot."

The nephew gave her a blank look. "I don't understand."

"I mean, the note wasn't in the carton with the parrot."

"Oh," said the man. "Oh, dear, that is very unfortunate. I hope everything worked out in the end."

"It did," said Bunny. "It was very nice to meet you." She rose to her feet and leaned over to kiss Aunt Fanny. "We'll be up to see you again soon. Finn and I have an appointment, so we'll have to say goodbye."

As they reached the door to the corridor, Bunny heard the nephew say behind her, to Aunt Fanny, "How did your young visitor know what happened to the parrot?" He sounded bewildered.

Aunt Fanny was not. Aunt Fanny was a shrewd old girl who still had all her marbles. "That young woman is not my friend. She's my niece."

Bunny closed the door behind her.

"Good lord, Bunny," said Finn. "That's where you got Saz. Mystery solved."

Bunny shook her head, smiling. "And it changed my life."

"Our lives. Just one thing." Finn stared at her.

She stared back.

They said it together. "Saz is not a guy."

"There goes my reverse harem," said Bunny glumly as Finn drove them in the new beige car back to their hotel. "It's more a ménage à trois."

"à quatre," said Finn. "Two of us. Two of you. I like the new arrangement."

"Remember how you told me I should give Saz a unisex name?" she said.

"No. Did I say that?"

"You did. You were right. You know, it works? Saz. Sazzie. Sassy," she tried. "What?"

"I'm always right." The smirk curling the corner of Finn's lip nettled her.

Not for long.

She wiped it off his face as soon as they got back to the hotel, so then she rocked a satisfied smirk of her own in the end.

Unwrapping the package

THE NEXT DAY, BUNNY and Finn got an early start back. Finn made her drive the beige car.

She didn't want to admit it, but the thing drove very smoothly. And Finn was right. It was small, smallish—not the behemoth the hotpinkmobile had been, for sure—but peppy.

Very soon they were pulling into the driveway off Beachcomber Road. There to greet them on the front porch was Ada, Bingo on his leash.

As Bunny got out of the car, she felt a bit panicky. Ada had what she could only describe as a snake-bit look.

"What happened?" Bunny gasped.

"Nothing bad," said Ada. "Just. Something strange."

Bunny rushed for Sazzie's cage. She stopped dead.

Sazzie was parading around the floor of the cage, bobbing his head.

HER head, Bunny reminded herself.

She was parading, preening herself, flaunting her feathers. She was showing off a cluster of small white eggs on the floor of the cage. Bunny counted them. Four.

"Saz!" Bunny screeched.

"Good birrrrd," Saz screeched back.

Finn set their suitcases down in the hall and came in to look, too. He began to laugh.

"But Finn. There's no Mister Saz. What the freak."

"Birds do that. Parrots do. A female parrot without a mate might lay a few eggs. Hard to know what it means, exactly. Could mean the bird's unhappy, but Saz? Naaah."

"Queenie?" Bunny tried softly.

Saz turned her head from side to side, looking at Bunny out of one eye, then the other. She didn't reply.

Bunny put her hand into the cage, and Saz stepped up. She preened Bunny, love-bit her, purred on her. "What the frak. Saz is a happy girl. I don't care what it means."

"Might check it out with Dr. Bekele, though."

"Maybe," said Bunny.

After sending Ada home, sending out for some Mervin and Bob's, having great welcome-home afternoon sex, Bunny at last got around to browsing through the mail.

A long white envelope arrested her attention.

She ripped it open and read the letter inside.

Finn had just come in from checking on the aviary. He caught sight of Bunny slumped on the sofa, reading through the letter and some accompanying papers.

"What's that."

"Uhh. There's something I've been meaning to tell you," said Bunny.

"Uh oh. What."

"Sit down." Bunny patted the poop-spotted sofa cushion beside her.

Finn sat.

"There's this program." Bunny suddenly felt shy.

"Tell me about it."

"It's at the University. The branch in Wilmington."

"Yeah?" Finn suddenly looked alert.

"I was thinking, uh."

"Yeah?" He gentled his tone, grabbed her hand and squeezed it.

She squeezed his hand back and then squeezed her eyes shut tight. "I thought maybe take some classes."

"Yes!" Finn shouted. He quieted down. "Yes," he said in a calmer voice. "That is a great idea, Bunny."

"I'm too old."

"You're not." After a moment, he said, "What classes? Continuing ed?"

"Uh."

He grabbed the letter out of her hand. "Wow, Bunny. This is an acceptance letter. You're gonna be a freshman in the university's B.S. program this fall. Wow. And three of your four community college classes transferred, too."

She looked at him pleadingly. "It was a whim, all right? I shouldn't actually do this. I'm too old."

"Bunny. You're not too old. These days there are plenty of adults going back to college. This is wonderful. It's not very far away. These days, you can probably do some of it online. And your profs will love you."

"They will not. I'm kinda dumb. They always said in high school, maybe get a secretarial certificate."

"You are not dumb. Your high school teachers or counselors or whoever told you that are dumb. Geez Louise, Bunny. I'm thinking of, like, finding an old Walkman or something, and recording "You are not dumb" into it, and you can just push the little red button so I don't have to keep saying it."

"I made a D in high school chemistry."

"We've established that. What were you doing, the semester you made the D?"

"Uh." Bunny thought back. "I had just broken up with the quarterback on the football team."

"See there?" He looked at her, exasperated. "And I nearly failed freshman comp and got sent home from college because woohoo, I was partying for the first time in my life and couldn't be bothered writing some paper using the five-paragraph argument. All that means is, education is wasted on the young. Or something. Or maybe." He paused and got a faraway look in his eyes. He put both hands together in prayer. "When you're ready to learn, the teacher will appear," he intoned.

"That's kinda profound, Finn."

"I thought so."

"So you think I should do it."

"Of course. What do you think you will study? It's okay not to know right away. Half the first couple years of college are exploring around to see what you want to do."

"I already know what I want to do. Study biology. Get through the early classes so I can take the ornithology course. That's about birds," she added.

"I know." He smirked.

"But suppose I fail chemistry."

"I'll tutor you."

"Suppose I fail. Like, FAIL, fail."

"Then you'll be a few years older with a lot more knowledge."

"A few years older and a lot poorer."

"You're an adult woman going back to college. There are scholarships for that. I'll help you find some." He nestled her close to him. "I'm really proud of you."

"You sound like my big brother, or my daddy."

"Let me rephrase that. I'm proud I know you. How's that?"

"I'll take that," said Bunny.

The nestling was just about to get more urgent when the doorbell burred.

"Dammit," said Finn. They got up to see who was there.

"Sarabeth!" said Finn.

The teenager clerk from UPWD stood before them in neatly pressed safari shorts and shirt.

"Hey, Finn! Hey, Bunny! They promoted me. I'm the UPWD's newest driver."

"Congratulations," Finn and Bunny said, practically together.

"And you have a package." Sarabeth produced a really small box and handed it over. She looked startled. "And, uh, another one, but the other one is really big."

Finn went out to the UPWD truck to help her get it in. When he returned, manhandling a very large carton, he was grinning from ear to ear. "My Surly!"

Finn and Bunny congratulated Sarabeth again on her promotion. Before she left, Bunny pressed a little sample tub of the Sazarac orangey tawny lipstick on her.

Finn moved the big carton into the front hall, and Bunny took charge of the tiny box. She took it back to the sofa.

"Oh, it's a package for you," said Bunny, handing it over. "Thought it might be some kinda parrot thing."

"Maybe it is," said Finn with a quirk of an eyebrow.

He made a big show of opening it up.

To reveal: a ring box.

He flipped it up. "Would you consider trading in your Crackerjacks ring for this, Miss Bunny Dowdy?"

"It's beautiful!" Bunny's eyes shone. The ring was white-gold, and a clever little gold parrot twined up one side. Set into the top of the ring, a very sparkly diamond.

Not a diamond like the Charlie Hope Diamond, but then, Bunny never was moved by that ring.

She was moved by this one.

"Except the answer is no," she said, "You're not taking my Crackerjacks ring. Ever. I'm keeping that. You'll have to bury it with me when I croak, like the fabled jewels of the Mysterious East that get buried with the pharaohs when they end up mummies."

"I'll agree to that," said Finn. "Try this one on."

The new ring fit perfectly.

"It was back-ordered," he said. "They make these specially. But when I thought about waiting to ask you to marry me until they could get it to me, I couldn't." He pulled her close and whispered it in her ear. "I couldn't wait, Bunny."

Much later, as the moon beamed into their bedroom window—Bunny's, now theirs—Finn told her the second part of his plan.

"The same custom jeweler is sending me two gold bands, one for each of us, and they each have parrots engraved on them. Too much?" He looked over at her anxiously.

Her eyes glowed in the moonlight. "Never too much."

"Beach wedding?"

"Oh, yes!"

"Bingo the ringbearer, with the rings tied onto his collar?"

"Yes!"

"Suppose he can't help himself and goes bounding into the surf?"

"He won't."

"Saz as. . .hmm. I was gonna make Saz my best man."

"He'll have to be the flower girl, that's all. And my two best friends will be my bridesmaids."

So they figured it all out together. They figured out their lives together, building in a lot of flex for the times life throws its curve balls.

"Whatever it takes, I'll be here for you," Finn whispered.

"But suppose—" Bunny began to worry.

"Shhh. Shhhh." Finn put a finger to her lips and stopped whatever she was about to say with a kiss.

Which led to another.

Which led to another, and some other things, and—

Below in the dark, dreaming house they could just hear Saz. "Good birrrrd," she was saying to herself sleepily. "Good girrrrrrl."

And soon, satisfied and smiling, Finn and Bunny were dreaming together themselves. The beach house rode the dream-surf underneath the light of the moon. In the morning, they opened their eyes to each other's smiles, to the rolling in of the waves up the beach, and they knew they'd never get enough of each other.

In their own way, good dog, good birrrrd, Bingo and Saz rushed to agree. And to bark and squawk until their two favorite humans rolled out of bed to play.

Please review this book on whatever e-book platform you use, on goodreads.com, and on any other sites or in any other groups where book lovers congregate. Bunny thanks you! Finn thanks you! Bingo thanks you! Sazzie thanks you! (and Lucinda thanks you a bunch). Like a Boss Red Rona. . .not so much.

ABOUT THE AUTHOR

Lucinda McFall

IS THE PEN NAME OF a transplanted Southeasterner who now splits her time between Minneapolis and the Sandia Mountains of New Mexico. You can find out about her books at https://lucindawritesromance.com. Sign up for her newsletter there, so you can get the latest news about her newest books.

Under her real name, Jane Wiseman, she writes fantasy and other speculative fiction. You can find out about those books at https://janemwiseman.com. She is also a published poet, and paints for fun with more enthusiasm than skill. And another thing. No matter what you call her, no matter what kinds of things she's writing, she misses the beach.

Don't miss out!

Visit the website below and you can sign up to receive emails whenever Lucinda McFall publishes a new book. There's no charge and no obligation.

https://books2read.com/r/B-A-SZVT-HMDBC

BOOKS 2 READ

Connecting independent readers to independent writers.

Did you love *Big Package for Bunny*? Then you should read *Karaoke Nite at the Love Club*[1] by Lucinda McFall!

[2]

When Gina and Doug stumble into an unlikely partnership at a coastal community's Karaoke Night, a sign challenges: Fall in Love! We Dare You! It's the Beach!

Gina is an artist. Doug is a golf pro. Could any two people be more different? Besides, they're both older, and both have hurting hearts.

Do they dare to act on the chemistry that sparks between them? A good doggie might have something to say about that. Hey, anything can happen. It's the beach!

---

1. https://books2read.com/u/4jgvPo

2. https://books2read.com/u/4jgvPo

Go to Lucinda's web site, https://lucindawritesromance, to find out more about this book and others in the Love's A Beach romance novel series.

Also by Lucinda McFall

Love's a Beach
Karaoke Nite at the Love Club
Big Package for Bunny
Storm Flags Flying, Deanie May

Tangled Web
That Fraudster Love